*THEIR WAY OF LIFE WAS BEING
STOLEN FROM THEM.
NOW THEY HAD TO FIGHT BACK.*

CHITTO HARJO, "CRAZY SNAKE": He faced death as a boy before the white soldiers' guns—now he rode toward it again as a man who had become a vanishing people's last hope. He told the Creeks to unite, he showed them how to be strong, and he taught them what courage and cunning could do. . . .

COKA CHUPKO: A Creek dwarf who was short of stature and large of heart. He saved the life of Crazy Snake, the boy, and became the loyal right hand of the man—but it was his hot-tempered shot that murdered an Oklahoma deputy and started a war. . . .

FAHNEE: The Creek Medicine Woman had not only the skill to heal Crazy Snake's wounds but also a plan that would lead to an ingenious escape, the daring to mislead the white lawmen, and the genius to leave behind an unsolved mystery about Crazy Snake's fate. . . .

SALINA JONES: For too few years she had a happy home near Tiger Mountain with her husband and sons. Proud to be Crazy Snake's wife, she never guessed that one day she could lose everything in a rampage against her people, and her husband. . . .

*Please turn the page to read the critics' praise
of Robert J. Conley. . . .*

Books by Robert J. Conley

*Published by POCKET BOOKS

CRAZY SNAKE

ROBERT J.
CONLEY

POCKET BOOKS

New York London Toronto Sydney Tokyo Singapore

This story is based upon actual events. However, some of the
characters and incidents portrayed herein are fictitious, and any
similarity to the name, character, or history of any person, living or
dead, or any actual event is entirely coincidental and unintentional.

An *Original* Publication of POCKET BOOKS

POCKET BOOKS, a division of Simon & Schuster Inc.
1230 Avenue of the Americas, New York, NY 10020

ISBN: 0-671-77902-8

First Pocket Books printing September 1994

10 9 8 7 6 5 4 3 2 1

POCKET and colophon are registered trademarks of
Simon & Schuster Inc.

Cover art by Tim Tanner

Printed in the U.S.A.

This book is respectfully dedicated to the memory of Louis "Littlecoon" Oliver and to Knokovtee Scott and all other descendants of the Loyal Creeks.

Introduction

The story of Chitto Harjo, called Crazy Snake in English, has fascinated me for a number of years, but since I'm a Cherokee, I have had a tendency to focus my own writings on Cherokee subjects. I never seriously considered writing about Chitto Harjo, who was Muskogee, or Creek, until a Creek friend of mine suggested it to me. I'm glad he did. The story is as fascinating as ever.

A few notes here at the beginning might be helpful to the reader. Throughout the text, except when the characters speaking or "thinking" are white people, I have referred to Chitto Harjo always by both names. Some historians, once they have identified him, will refer to him from then on as Harjo or as Snake as if the second name were an English-type surname. That is not the case.

Chitto is "snake." *Harjo* is the word that is translated into English as "crazy." In the Creek language the adjective follows the noun. The name is not, therefore, a combination of surname and given name. It's one name.

Creek naming practice in the old days was to give a man a name that consisted of, first, the name of his clan or perhaps a place name, the name of his community. In the case of Chitto Harjo, it seems to have been a clan name, for the Creeks do have a snake clan. The second name then was sometimes a war title or some other kind of earned name, and *harjo* means something like "recklessly brave." In English it's "crazy."

The reader should not be confused, therefore, at finding other characters in the tale who are also known as recklessly brave. Chotch Harjo, for example, was not, as far as I know, related to Chitto Harjo.

Details in the life of Chitto Harjo are still being disputed by historians. Perhaps the most argued about is the time and manner of his death. The reader will find some of the characters in this novel putting forth various theories that are still being debated. As a writer of historical fiction, I have made my choice based on what seems reasonable to me and which version I prefer as well as which version is preferred by my Creek friends.

I would like to acknowledge here the valuable help of several friends in the preparation of this work. Knokovtee Scott, Frankie Sue Gilliam, and Art Burton especially provided me with important details and insights in various conversations and with material from their own files.

CREEK NATION
Indian Territory
1890

Osages   Cherokees

TULSA
• BROKEN ARROW

• COWETA

Cimarron

Arkansas River

Verdigris River

FORT GIBSON

Deep Fork of Canadian River

NUYAKA

☆ OKMULGEE

MUSKOGEE

HENRYETTA

OKTAHA

Tiger Mt.
CHECOTAH

Hickory Ground

North Fork of Canadian River

Missouri Pacific

Cherokees

EUFAULA

Seminoles

Wewoka Creek

Canadian River

Choctaws

Chicka-saws

M. JACOB 1954

Flight to Kansas

1861

1

He was fourteen years old, and he did not fully understand what was happening around him. He knew that there were major events of immense proportions taking place, not just in the Muskogee or Creek Nation, his home, but in the larger world outside, a world in which he had no experience, very little actual knowledge, and no control whatsoever.

He knew about the United States, of course. The people were always talking about the United States. That was where the white people came from. It was the place where lived the men who could issue orders to the Creek Nation, and the Creek people had to obey.

He had heard the old men talk about a time when the Creeks had fought a war against the white men of the United States. They had fought against a white man named Andrew Jackson. The leader of

3

the Creeks had been Lumhi Chati, a great man. Lumhi Chati, Red Eagle, had been called William Weatherford by the white men, and because the Cherokees had joined forces with the white men, the Creeks had been soundly defeated. Red Eagle had surrendered to Jackson, and Jackson had forced him to sign a bad treaty.

He had also heard the old men and old women talk about the long trail of tears, the time when the white men had forced the Creek people to leave their homelands back in the east and make the journey to new western lands. It had been a bad trip. Many people had died along the way. The Creeks had not been asked if they wanted to make the move. They had been forced to do it. And it had been the same Andrew Jackson who had caused it to happen.

He had heard all those stories. But the move had been made under a treaty, and the white men had promised, with the treaty, that if the Creeks would move to the West, they would not be bothered again. They would be far away from the white man. Safe out there in the West, they would have their own government, make their own laws.

All these stories, he had heard. He had never seen the country in the East, for the removal had taken place before his birth. Sometimes he tried to imagine what the old land was like. Sometimes he thought that he would like to see it someday, but he imagined, from what he had heard, that it was full of white people, and he thought that he would be afraid to go visit there.

Andrew Jackson was dead, and the Creek Nation had a sacred treaty, a paper on which solemn promises made by both sides were recorded. Representatives from both sides had signed their names to the paper, and the paper said that the Creeks would never again be bothered in their own land.

But things were happening in the United States that were causing new problems for the Creeks. He didn't fully understand the things that were happening, but he had heard the old men talking. Some white men had come among them from outside. These men had said that they were separating themselves from the United States. They said that there would no longer be a United States, and that, when the United States was no more, the old treaty would be no good.

They said that there would be a new power, a new white man's government, and it would be called the Confederate States of America, and if the Creeks wanted to be safe in their lands, they should sign a new treaty with the representatives of the Confederate States.

The proposal from the Confederates was considered by the Creek government. The Creek Nation was divided into two major districts, the Arkansas District, or Lower Towns, and the Canadian District, or Upper Towns. Each district provided the national government with a Principal Chief and a Second Chief, and there was a national legislature of two houses, the House of Warriors and the House of Kings.

There were also political factions that had devel-

oped, largely because of intermarriages between
Creeks and whites. These marriages had resulted in
a large mixed-blood population within the Creek
Nation, and the mixed-bloods tended to think
more like white people than like Creeks. They were
called "progressives." The full-bloods were called
"conservatives" or sometimes "traditionals." Often, they were also called backward.

At the council meeting, the men had said, the
Confederates had convinced the mixed-bloods, and
the mixed-bloods had managed to convince some
of the full-bloods. When the final vote was counted,
the council had decided to sign a new treaty with
the new Confederate States.

But Chief Oktarharsas (Sandy Place) Harjo had
walked away from the meeting in disgust, and many
of the full-bloods had followed him. Oktarharsas
Harjo had said that as far as he knew, the old
United States still existed, and therefore the old
treaty was still in effect. He and his followers, he
had said, would be loyal to the old promises they
had made, loyal to the old treaty, loyal to the
United States. People began to call him and his
followers the Loyal Creeks.

Chebon, the boy, was only fourteen years old,
and he did not quite understand all of the things
that were happening. But he heard the men talking,
the old men, and they said that the Confederates
had signed treaties with the Choctaws and the
Chickasaws and the Seminoles, even with the Cherokees. They had also signed with some of the
smaller tribes to the north, the Osages, Quapaws,

and Senecas. Out west, they had signed treaties with some of the wild tribes, and the two nearest states, Arkansas and Texas, had both become Confederate.

He could tell by the somber tones of their voices and by the expressions on their faces that his elders were becoming more and more fearful, that they were worried for the safety of themselves and their families and for the future of their nation. He heard them say that the mission schools had been closed and the children had all been sent home. And he heard that many Creeks, mostly the mixed-blood, progressive, slaveholding Creeks, the ones who lived like white men and, more often than not, looked like white men, had become soldiers in the Army of the Confederate States of America.

Then came the day his father had taken the whole family in their wagon to a large council meeting of the Loyal Creeks. Oktarharsas Harjo had been there, as well as the great Opothle Yahola, the man who had been the leader of the Creeks back in the old country, who had fought to keep the old land and then, when there was no more hope, had led them west to their new land. He wore a silver medal on his chest that had been given him by Millard Fillmore, President of the United States, almost ten years earlier.

At the council meeting it was said that the treaty with the Confederate States was illegal, and therefore their own government, which had signed it, was illegal. They declared that they, the Loyal Creeks, were the legal government of the Creek

Nation, and they elected Oktarharsas Harjo Principal Chief.

"And so that we'll all know each other no matter where we meet," said the new chief, "we'll each wear a corn-shuck badge right here." He patted himself on the left side of his chest.

Then someone came and said that Chief Canard, the mixed-blood chief of the Confederate Creeks, had placed a bounty of $5,000 on the head of Oktarharsas Harjo.

It was a few days later when the boy heard that Oktarharsas Harjo and Opothle Yahola had together sent a letter to Abraham Lincoln, the President of the United States. He heard the men talking about what had been said in the letter. They had reminded the President of the treaty that had sent them to the West and taken all of their eastern lands, and they reminded him of the promise that had been made that they would never again be molested in their new lands.

Then they told Mr. Lincoln that they needed his help and advice. "The wolf has come," they said. They said that strangers had come among them, trying to make them fight against the United States. "Our children are frightened," they wrote, "and the mothers cannot sleep for fear." Then they asked the President to "send us word what to do." The letter concluded with the following words: "I am alive. I well remember the treaty. My ears are open and my memory is good."

Then the boy's father had said that they were moving. They packed all of their belongings into their wagon and hitched the wagon to a team of mules. They gathered their few head of cattle, and because he was fourteen years old, a big boy, he walked, driving the cattle, while the rest of the family rode in the wagon, his father handling the reins.

They went to a place on the Little River where other families of Loyal Creeks had already gathered, and there they camped. Some of them built lean-tos, arbors, or other kinds of temporary shelter. Some few had canvas tents. Others simply slept on the ground, some under their wagons, some out in the open. They cooked over open campfires, and they shared their food with each other. They also had another big council meeting there.

This time, like-minded people from other tribes, including some Cherokees, Chickasaws, and Seminoles, showed up and took part in the discussion, and all of them who stayed, and nearly all of them did, fastened corn-shuck badges to their breasts.

The fourteen-year-old *chebon* did not understand all that was said. He still did not know why all this was happening. He did deeply resent the fact that someone or something had thrown his young life into chaos.

His first fourteen years had been happy, carefree ones. His family was a good one, close. He did his share of work around the house, and he ran in the woods with other boys his age. Often his father took him along to hunt. It had been a good life, and it seemed unjust, even almost unreal, that these things were happening.

He became aware that the new council of the Loyal Creeks had sent three men, Micco Hutke (or White Chief), Bob Deer, and Joe Ellis, to Kansas with the letter to the President, and he heard people talking about the dangers they were likely to encounter along the way.

"Do you think they'll make it?" someone asked. "Will our letter get through?"

"I don't know. There's all those rebels out there. All around us."

"And outlaws. Especially up around the border between the Cherokee Nation and Kansas. Bad men hang out there. They break the laws in Kansas and then run across the border into the Cherokee Nation."

"Micco Hutke's a smart man. He can figure out how to get through."

"And Bob Deer can fight if he has to."

"So can the other two. They can all fight."

"But there are only three of them. They might not get through."

Along with the adults, the fourteen-year-old worried about the safety of the three men, and he worried about the success of their mission. He did not know what the President would do when he received the letter, but he had gotten the impression from things he had overheard that the letter would somehow solve all their problems. He prayed that the letter would make it safely to a place called Washington.

It seemed to him a long time before the men returned to the camp of the Loyal Creeks, and he tried to press himself to the front of the crowd during the meeting when the men made their report. He managed to hear most of the story that way, and he was able to pick up the rest in bits of conversation that followed the meeting.

The men had made it all the way to the Shawnee Agency in Kansas, where the agent had promised that he would forward their letter to Washington. Then they had made arrangements with the agent for a meeting to take place in Kansas between a Federal agent and representatives of the Loyal Creeks.

It was almost three months later, though, when the meeting finally took place. During that long wait, the boy felt as if time were standing still. He had spent the first fourteen years of his life in a log house with a fireplace. He had a bed in a loft in that house. And he had lived there with his family and with a sense of perfect security. At Little River, with the Loyal Creeks, he was living in a temporary camp. It was crowded, noisy, and unsanitary. He was nervous, even scared, all of the time, and he desperately wanted his old life back. He had begun to believe, though, that he would never get it back.

The same three men had gone back to Kansas for the meeting, but they had been accompanied this time by some Seminoles and Chickasaws. By the time they returned to the camp on Little River, it was late November. It was cold.

They reported that they had at last met with an

agent for the Creeks. They believed that, because all of their old agents had gone with the Confederacy, the United States had appointed a new agent for them and had sent him to Kansas.

They had told this new agent their problems, and they had told him of their loyalty. They had reminded him of the terms of the old treaty and assured him that they intended to continue to live by its promises. They asked him for a U.S. Army escort back to their people, telling him that it was not safe for them in the Cherokee Nation, through which they had to travel, or even in their own Creek Nation. They also asked for ammunition, clothing, tents, and their annuities, due them by terms of the treaty.

Instead, the agent had sent them to Washington, a long ride on a railroad train. In Washington some men had taken them to see the powerful U.S. Army marching up and down. Then the men took them to see President Lincoln himself.

"We told him," said Micco Hutke, "of the trouble we're having here, and he told us that our treaties are good and will be respected. Then he said he'll send us help as soon as he can."

It was the answer they had all been hoping for, and they rejoiced at the news. Even the camp didn't seem quite so bad anymore to the boy, for now it seemed that there would be an end to it after all. The President of the United States would send the great U.S. Army, and the Loyal Creeks would all be taken safely back to their homes. Surely the great U.S. Army, the army that had defeated Lumhi

Chati in the Red Stick War, the army that had been able to move all of the Indians west across the Mississippi River, surely that same army would take care of these Confederates in short order, and peace and the proper way of life would be restored in the Creek Nation.

— 2 —

The joy was short-lived. The hoped-for aid did not come. Time continued to pass slowly, and the Confederate forces in the Creek Nation continued to organize and to build up their strength. A Creek Confederate regiment was raised under the command of Colonel Daniel N. McIntosh, half brother to old Chilly McIntosh, who had signed the removal treaty in Georgia back in 1824.

The new Confederate States of America had established a Department of the Indian Territory to cover not only the Creek Nation but also the Chickasaw Nation, the Choctaw Nation, the Seminole Nation, the Cherokee Nation, and the smaller nations to the north, the Osage, the Quapaw, the Seneca.

And placed in command of the whole operation was Albert Sidney Pike. A huge white man with a long gray beard and serious political ambitions,

Pike was a flamboyant dresser and a bombastic speaker, and he fancied himself a poet. He was not, however, in control of his new post. Having negotiated his treaties with the several Indian tribes, he had gone to the Confederate capital at Richmond. In his absence, another white man named Douglas Cooper had assumed command of the Confederate Indian Territory troops.

Before the secession of the southern states, Cooper had been the Federal agent to the Creek Nation. He had been the man to whom the Creeks would turn with their problems. Now, to the Loyal Creeks, he represented the enemy, and with the massive troop buildup in Indian Territory, he had become a real threat.

The problems facing the Loyal Creeks had suddenly become tactical rather than political, and without making any formal announcements to the general assembly there at Little River, Oktarharsas Harjo simply and quietly stepped back out of the way to allow Opothle Yahola to take command. The old chief immediately ordered the breaking up of the camp.

The fourteen-year-old boy was glad to hear the order. He did not know where they were going, but he was sick of the stinking camp at Little River. And he was weary and bored from the tedium of camp life. Anything would be a welcome relief. He helped his family pack the wagon again, and he herded up their remaining cattle. Most of them had already been slaughtered and eaten. There were many people to be fed in the camp.

Other families were equally busy gathering what

few belongings they had managed to bring with them to Little River. People chased cows and pigs. Mothers collected their children. Dogs barked. In the midst of all this confusion, Opothle Yahola moved about issuing orders, giving advice and encouragement. He alone seemed to know exactly what he was doing and what needed to be done. He alone seemed calm and assured. He was in command, and he was in control.

The boy had never before paid much attention to Opothle Yahola. He had met many revered old men, and he had always shown the proper respect and deference. But here at Little River, with so many people . . . How many were there? he wondered. There were hundreds, he was sure. Maybe a thousand or more.

The old man had taken charge. He was clearly in control of the situation. Opothle Yahola seemed to take on a new stature in the eyes of the boy as he rode up and down the long line of wagons on the back of his fine black stallion. He seemed to lose some of his years. His back seemed straighter. His voice was strong and sure, and his dark eyes flashed. Or so thought the boy who hurried his father's cattle along as best he could.

The boy was amazed at how soon the wagon train began to roll. There were many buckboards, a few covered wagons, and even a buggy here and there. Some people rode horseback. Many walked. Cattle were driven along beside the wagons or behind them, and some people did their best to drive hogs along. Those people seemed to be the busiest. The hogs seemed to resist the herding, each wanting to run off in its own direction. Dogs ran back and forth along the length of the train, barking and nipping at the feet of the horses and mules. Some pestered the cattle and the hogs. Some ran off to chase rabbits, only to rejoin the caravan later, their tongues hanging long out of their mouths.

It was cold. People with coats pulled them close around themselves and fastened them tight. Others wore blankets wrapped around their shoulders and their heads. Still others did without and simply endured the cold as best they could. They had no other choice.

They traveled east and slightly north. The boy never did understand where they were going or why. He didn't much care. He was glad to have left behind the overused campsite on the Little River. Perhaps they were only moving because of the condition of the camp, he thought, but he didn't really believe that. There had been too great a sense of urgency in the packing and leaving. There had been the abrupt change of command from Oktarharsas Harjo to Opothle Yahola. Something was up. He was sure of that. But he wasn't sure what it would turn out to be.

The slow-moving wagon train traveled for five days before Opothle Yahola called a halt. They had reached the place where the North Fork of the Canadian River and Deep Fork came together, and there they established a hasty and temporary camp. Opothle Yahola told them to prepare for a long trip. His intention, he said, was to lead them to the safety of Kansas, where the Union troops held sway. They would have to travel north out of the

Creek Nation and through the Cherokee Nation in order to reach Kansas. There would be danger of attack from the Indian Confederates all along the way.

The people slaughtered cattle and hogs and prepared the meat. They readied what weapons they had. Some had old rifles and pistols. Many had bows and arrows. Some had nothing but sticks or farm tools. And while they were thus involved, others came into the camp to join them. The newcomers were not all Creek.

There were Seminoles, Kickapoos, Shawnees, Delawares, and Wichitas, even Comanches! The numbers grew until the boy thought that the hundreds must have become a few thousand. Certainly in his fourteen years he had never been a part of such a gathering or such a movement.

Opothle Yahola seemed tireless. His advanced age did not appear to hinder him at all in his duties. He moved around among the people, checking on their progress, seeing if they needed anything, helping when and where he could. When the boy, now really a young man, felt discouraged or tired or bored, he looked to the old leader for inspiration, and he was not disappointed, not ever. The young spirit seemed to draw strength from the old one.

The boy helped with the slaughtering of hogs and cattle. He cut and carried wood. When he was done with his own chores, he helped his neighbors with theirs, and since many of his neighbors were people he had not known before, he made many new friends. There was always work to be done, and there was constant anxiety. Still, it was better than the seemingly endless camp life back at Little River.

He was aware that Opothle Yahola had sent out some scouts. He did not know exactly what they were scouting for. He assumed that they were on the lookout for Confederate soldiers. Now and then, as he went about his daily chores, the boy wondered about the scouts. He wondered where they were and what, if anything, they had seen, and he wondered when they would return, bringing news. He had also begun to wonder if the Confederate soldiers would actually attack them. He wondered if he would have to fight, and if so, what kind of a warrior he would make.

They sat around a small fire beside their wagon, the boy, his sister, and his mother. His father was off talking with other men. They had eaten a meal of boiled pork and fried bread and coffee. It was dark, and the night was cold.

"Are we going to stay here, Mother?" asked the girl.

"I don't know, Polly," said the mother. "I don't think so. Not for very long anyway."

"When will we go home?"

"I don't know that either. Maybe we won't go home. Maybe we'll have to live somewhere else. It seems like Indians always have to move somewhere."

"But the United States Army will whip these Confederates, won't it?" said the boy.

"I don't know. They don't seem to care what's happening to us here. They don't seem to be interested in us at all."

"But we have a treaty with them," said the boy. "I heard the men talking about it. They're supposed to send the army here to protect us. They promised in the treaty."

"They don't care about that," said the mother. "They broke their promises before. Lots of times. They only make us keep our treaty promises to them. They don't care about keeping the ones they make to us."

"Are we going to Kansas, then?" he asked.

"I think so. I don't know when. It will be a long trip for so many people to make. I don't know how long it will take us to get there."

"Do you think we'll have to fight along the way?"

"I'm afraid of that," his mother answered. "Until this trouble started, I thought that the wars were all behind us. We stopped fighting the white men, and I didn't think that we'd have to fight anymore. Now the white men are having a war between themselves, and they've gotten us involved in it. It's not even our war. It's theirs. It's too bad, the way they do us Indians."

"If we fight," the boy said, "we'll be fighting other Creeks, won't we?"

"Yes. And other Indians. Cherokees and Choctaws and some others. And maybe some whites too."

He glanced across the fire at his mother's face. It was a troubled face, a sad face. He wondered what she was thinking, but of course, he couldn't know.

How could a fourteen-year-old boy know what was in a mother's heart, a mother who was contemplating the approach of battle in which she could lose her husband and her children?

Could she read his thoughts? He was afraid, but he would never admit it, not even to her. He hated having to admit it to himself. He had never had to fight before, to fight for his life, fight to kill. He wondered if he would kill. What would it feel like to kill another human being, perhaps another Creek person? Would it change him forever? And if it did, how would he be changed?

And then he had another thought, one that had not occurred to him before. He wondered if he would be one of the ones to die. He wondered what it would feel like to have a bullet tear through his flesh. He guessed that it wouldn't be so bad if it killed him at once. But what if it did not? What if it left him to die a slow and lingering death? Or worse yet, what if it left him alive but crippled and helpless? He decided that he would rather be dead than helpless. He lay awake a long time that night with these same thoughts troubling his mind.

The next day the scouts returned. They came riding hard into camp, hurrying to see Opothle Yahola. They jumped from the backs of their horses, leaving others to catch up with and take care of the sweating, panting animals. They ran up to their leader. Others rushed over to try to hear what the scouts had to report. There was a hurried conversation, and then an announcement was made for all the people to gather around. Opothle Yahola climbed up onto a wagon so that all could see him, and he spoke in a voice both loud and clear.

"As you can see," he said, "our scouts have returned. They bring word that Agent Cooper is coming with Confederate troops. Some of the troops are Indian and some are Texans. They know where we are, and they think that we're organized to fight them on behalf of the United States. They don't believe that we want to stay out of this and be left alone. They're coming here to attack us.

"We could stay and fight them, but most of us have our families here with us. We're going north. We'll try to outrun them, try to avoid them and get to Kansas. The United States Army is in Kansas, and there we'll be safe from the war. We'll wait it out up there, and when the United States has finally put down this rebellion, we'll be able to return to our homes.

"Now let's get packed and ready to go. There's no time to waste."

They had gone through it before, and they were loaded, lined up, and actually moving north in a very short time. The train was bigger than it had been before, much bigger. More people had joined them along the way. There were a few more wagons, many more horses, and many more people on foot. As before, Opothle Yahola moved back and forth along the line, constantly checking on the people, making sure that everything was all right, that no one slowed them down and no one got left behind.

They moved north, a confusion of people and horses, mules and cattle, hogs and dogs. There was a wild array of costume and a babble of tongues, but there was also the ever-present confidence-inspiring figure of Opothle Yahola watching over all.

There was also the uncertainty of the future, the unknown land to the north, the adequacy or lack thereof of their food supply, the unpredictability of the winter weather, the possibility of Confederate troops anywhere along the way, and the definite, known pursuit of those behind. There was one question in the minds of all, a question that no one could answer. Would they make it to the safety of Kansas?

3

They had been traveling north for two weeks. It was the nineteenth of November when they camped for the night at Round Mountain near the place where the Arkansas and Cimarron Rivers came together. A cold wind was blowing in from the north. They had built their campfires and were ready to settle in for the night when the scouts came riding in.

"They're coming," shouted one of the scouts. "They're right behind us."

"How many?" asked Opothle Yahola.

"About a thousand, I'd say. Chilly McIntosh is leading the column, riding in his buggy. The first bunch of soldiers are white men. Texans, I think. Behind them are Indians. Mostly Creek. Mixed-bloods. They'll be on top of us by full dark."

Opothle Yahola began shouting orders, and the people scurried to comply. The camp was on the edge of a woods, and he sent the women and children into the woods to hide. Then he called up the men with rifles and had them take up places behind trees. Then the men with bows and arrows were placed. Among them was the fourteen-year-old boy about to face the first real fight of his life, about to find out what kind of a warrior he would make. His father was armed with the family's one rifle.

The fires were left burning, but no one was near them. In the dark, Opothle Yahola reasoned, the Confederates would rush toward the fires, yelling and shooting.

The young man took his place behind a tree. To his right and to his left were men with rifles. He couldn't see them, but he knew they were there. He held the bow in his left hand, an arrow in his right. His other arrows were close by his right hand. Already it was darker than it had been when the scouts had come in with the news.

He could see no one approaching from the southern horizon, and he wondered if the scouts had been right about the intention of the Confederates they had seen. Everyone was quiet, and he could feel, thought he could hear, his own heart beating. He wondered if anyone else could hear it. He wondered where his father was hidden and whether his mother and sister were far enough into the woods to be safe from danger.

Then all of a sudden he saw them and heard

them, more men on horseback than he had ever seen before, and they were racing their horses toward the campfires. Many of them waved sabers in the air. Others held rifles or pistols ready. They all seemed to be screaming at once. He felt a moment of panic, almost a wave of terror, and something inside him wanted to turn and run into the dark woods. Instead he took a deep breath and, his hands trembling, he nocked his arrow. He wondered if he was trembling from the cold or from fear. He waited.

He thought that he should hear a command to shoot from Opothle Yahola. But he didn't know where his leader was, and the attacking Confederate soldiers were making so much noise that he knew he wouldn't have been able to hear a command had it been given. Suddenly he saw arrows flying, and he took quick aim and let his own fly. He grabbed another and readied it.

Down among the campfires, arrows were raining on the Texans. Men and horses screamed. Some of the gray-suited Texans fired wildly. Then the riflemen fired from behind their trees. The Texans who had not been hit, and whose horses had not been disabled, turned to retreat. The young man loosed his second arrow and saw it hit a fleeing Texan low in the back. The attack seemed to be over almost as quickly as it had begun. Then he heard the voice of Opothle Yahola.

"Hold your places. Reload your weapons. They'll come again."

He picked up another arrow and held it ready.

He could hear all around him the sounds of men loading rifles. He strained his eyes out into the darkness, but he could not see the soldiers. He knew they were out there somewhere.

They came again. When some of them got in close to the fires, the young man could see that they were Indians. It was the second wave. Like the first, they were hit with a shower of arrows. As they turned to retreat, they were hit by a volley of rifle shots. There were stragglers, men who had been unhorsed, running, trying to catch up with their retreating comrades, and some of the Loyal Creeks raced out of the woods brandishing war clubs, short axes, knives, using rifles as clubs. They ran after the Confederates who had retreated on foot and chased them down, bashing in their heads as they caught up to them.

Opothle Yahola was shouting orders, but it took him a while to get the attention of everyone. At last, though, the ones who had run out of the woods came back, and everyone quieted down so they could hear what he had to say. The command was quick and clear.

"We're moving out," he said.

Supplies were abandoned in their hasty departure. Even a few wagons were left behind. The young man started to go after the few cows that were left to his family, but his father called out to him.

"Leave them," he said. "Get up in the wagon."

"Leave the cows?"

"Come on, boy."

He climbed up on the seat beside his father, and they lurched forward, and they were moving away from the fires, into the darkness.

"Why are we leaving?" he asked. "We beat them. Twice."

"We surprised them in the dark," said his father, "but they have more fighting men than we do, and they have more rifles and ammunition. If we stayed in that camp, they'd attack us in the morning. We're getting away from them. It's the smartest thing to do. It's what Opothle Yahola said."

On December 9 they reached the south bank of Bird Creek in the Cherokee Outlet. They were tired and hungry and cold. Opothle Yahola knew that the pursuers were getting close again. His scouts had reported to him that they would not be able to outrun the Confederates, and so he had called a halt to set up his defenses and prepare for the inevitable attack.

He lined up the wagons in a long arc, with the wagon on each end of the line close to the water. The attack would be coming from the south. It would not be as easy as the last time. It was daylight, and he knew that Cooper had been joined by other forces. His scouts thought that they were probably Cherokee Confederates. The Loyal Creeks were badly outnumbered.

The men with weapons placed themselves behind the wagons, some behind nearby trees, and waited. The young man had a position near the middle of the wagons. If the Confederates came straight at them, he would be one of the first to shoot. He was armed still with only his bow and a few arrows. He hoped the arrows would last through the fight.

His father, with the rifle, was not far from him, down the line to his right. His mother and sister were with the other women and children, back behind him in the trees along the bank of Bird Creek.

Silence hung heavily in the cold air. He could hear the sounds of his own breathing, and each time he exhaled, a puff of vapor shot out of his mouth like smoke. Then he heard the sounds of hundreds of horses, at first a low, distant rumble. It grew louder and louder, and then he saw them. They appeared on the far horizon, and the line of mounted men stretched as far as he could see in either direction.

They stopped there on the line between earth and sky, and the boy waited for the attack. It did not come. They sat there on the backs of their horses, just looking. Then he saw a horseman ride out, down the line and in again. He appeared to be having a conference with another horseman. In another moment, the rider held up a saber with a white cloth tied to its end. He rode alone toward the wagons. The boy tensed.

"Everyone hold your fire," shouted Opothle Yahola. "He wants to talk."

The old man climbed over a wagon tongue and took a few steps out away from the wagons, toward the approaching horseman. Another man stepped outside the arc of wagons to stand beside the leader of the Loyal Creeks. The rider stopped right in front of the two Creeks.

The boy couldn't hear what they were saying, but they talked for a moment. Then the rider dismounted. Opothle Yahola gestured back toward the wagons, and all three men crossed over the barricade. The man with the white flag was wearing a gray uniform, but he was an Indian. The boy could tell that. He could also tell, now that they were closer, that Opothle Yahola was talking to the man through an interpreter, the man who had gone to join him outside the wagons. Opothle Yahola seemed to be showing the man around, and he made a special point, it seemed, to take the man over to the area where the western Indians were waiting.

The boy noticed then that almost all of the western Indians were painted wildly. The Confederate Indian talked some more to Opothle Yahola, then shook his hand and walked back toward the wagons. He climbed over the barricade, walked to his horse, and mounted. Then he rode back toward the horizon.

"What's happening?" the boy heard someone say.

"That was Colonel Drew," said Opothle Yahola. "He's a Cherokee Confederate. I told him we were only trying to get out of here. We want to stay out of this white man's war. He said that he won't fight us, but the Texans will. Be ready now."

The boy watched as Colonel Drew joined the others on the far horizon. There seemed to be a brief conference out there, then the colonel rode his horse through the ranks. Others turned their mounts and followed him away. There were still a vast number of soldiers out there, but not quite so many as before.

Then there was a shout, a single voice that was almost immediately joined by hundreds of other voices, and the riders on the horizon came racing toward the wagons. The boy's heart thrilled, and he nocked an arrow. He heard shots and saw puffs of smoke. The attackers were firing. Then he heard louder shots coming from close by. The Loyal Creeks were returning the fire. He saw some of the attacking riders fall from their horses, saw some of the horses stumble and fall. Then some were close enough, and he took aim and let fly his arrow. It struck a rider in the thigh. He nocked another arrow, but before he could decide on a new target, the riders had turned and were racing away.

They gathered again on the horizon. They were not in full retreat. They would attack again. He glanced to his right down the line, and he saw a man there lying on his back on the ground. He felt a moment of panic, wondering if it could be his father. His father was down that direction, he knew. He straightened up, thinking to run over there and look, but just then he heard the strong voice of Opothle Yahola.

"Keep your places. Stay ready. They'll attack again."

He kept his place, but he kept looking in the direction of the fallen man. Then he saw his father. He was on his feet. He was not the fallen man. With a sigh of relief, the boy settled back into position and watched the horizon.

The soldiers up there were back in line, reorganized. They would likely attack again soon. Between them and the wagons, the landscape was littered with fallen men and horses, some dead, some dying. Men groaned, and hurt horses screamed in confusion and pain.

Then the chorus of rebel yells sounded again, and again the line rushed down toward the wagons. Saber blades gleamed in the sun, and puffs of smoke came from the barrels of guns. The boy nocked an arrow. The man nearest him to his left fired a rifle, and the loud report startled the boy. He looked for a target.

A rebel soldier seemed to be riding straight toward him. He was waving a saber over his head and yelling. The boy aimed and loosed his arrow. It sank into the horse's shoulder, and the horse screamed and shied. The man fell on his back. He scrambled to his feet and fell again as a rifle ball struck him in the chest.

The boy readied another arrow but dropped it as a bullet smashed into the wagon just by his head. He picked up the arrow and nocked it. Looking up, he saw at least a dozen men within his range. Quickly he picked one and loosed his arrow. It sank into the man's left shoulder. Suddenly the Confederates turned again and began their retreat. This time they did not stop at the horizon. They kept going. They disappeared. The boy wondered if it was some kind of trick.

Opothle Yahola must have had the same question in his mind, for he sent out the two scouts. The boy watched the two riders vanish in the trail of the retreating rebels. They were gone a long time, it seemed. Some of the men went out into the field and clubbed to death the wounded they found there. They also picked up all the sabers and all the guns and ammunition.

At last the scouts returned. They had a quick conference with Opothle Yahola. Then the old man climbed up on a wagon to make a general announcement.

"They're gone," he said. "We've driven them off for now. We have to start moving again. We have to get to Kansas as fast as we can."

As they moved out, the boy could see that a few wagons had been overturned. He wondered what the fighting had been like where that had happened, and he wondered what had become of the man he had seen lying on the ground. He didn't know if the man had been dead or merely hurt. He supposed that someone had put him in a wagon.

He sat beside his father on the wagon seat and rode for a while in silence, relieved to be back with his family and to know that they were all unhurt. Finally he spoke.

"Father," he said, "will they be back again?"

"They'll probably tend their wounded and bury their dead," said the father. "They'll get some reinforcements if they can and more supplies, more ammunition. Then they'll try again."

4

The wagons moved agonizingly slow, groaning and creaking in the cold air. Everyone knew that the Texas Confederates would attack again. They were still several days' travel from their goal of the Kansas border. Quietly and to himself, the boy wondered, even then, would the Kansas border actually stop the dreaded Confederate pursuit?

A wagon broke down, its wheel off. The occupants climbed down and hurriedly unhitched their horses. They continued moving, some on the backs of the draft animals, some on foot. There was no time to stop and repair a broken wagon wheel. The wagon and everything in it was abandoned, left for the rebels or other scavengers to pick at. The owners of the wagon did not look back. Along with the rest of the Loyal Creeks, they kept moving doggedly along the trail toward the sanctuary of Kansas.

Mounted scouts rode out ahead and behind to watch for danger, riding back in occasionally to report to Opothle Yahola on what they had seen. Other scouts were out on both flanks. Opothle Yahola would not let them be caught by surprise.

They had been seventeen days on the trail since the battle at Bird Creek, and they were dangerously low on supplies of all kinds, including ammunition. No one said anything, but they must have all been hoping the same hope: that they would reach their goal in Kansas before the rebels hit them again.

As they moved farther north, they found the ground covered with hard-packed snow. A bitter cold wind blew out of the northwest, and it seemed to be carrying tiny snowflakes with it through the air. The boy had already noticed that all of the creeks they had seen the last few days had been frozen.

Many of the people were sick, and he himself had developed an annoying cough. Cracking the ice, they crossed another low creek. Ahead of them, for about four hundred yards, stretched a nearly flat, open prairie. It was covered with snow. Beyond the prairie, hills rose, their sides covered with rocks and boulders.

The wagon in which the boy and his family rode had gone about halfway across the open prairie. Opothle Yahola was riding back alongside the wagons, checking to see that everyone was getting along all right. He was beside the wagon of the boy's family when the scout came racing up, and the boy was able to listen to the hurried conversation that took place between the two men.

"Cooper's right behind us," said the scout, "and he's got more men. About a thousand more, I'd say. And there's more coming up the Verdigris River to join him. More than a thousand there. They're mostly all white."

"How soon will they catch up with us, do you think?" asked the old chief.

"We'll be lucky if we make it across this clearing," said the scout. "They're right on top of us."

"You ride back to the rear and hurry them along back there," said Opothle Yahola. "I'm going on up to the front of the train. We'll make it to that hillside up ahead. Let's go."

Suddenly all the drivers were shouting and lashing at their animals. Wagons, horseback riders, and people on foot raced for the hillside. Wagons turned over in their haste, and runners slipped and fell in the snow. Children screamed and cried. Dogs ran barking in circles. There was no longer any attempt at keeping track of cattle or hogs. Nearly all of them had been left far behind by this time. They had probably been found, killed, and eaten by Confederates, the boy thought.

He could see, up ahead of him, the people who first reached the hillside jumping from their wagons or their saddles or the bare backs of their horses or mules and running for cover with their weapons. As his own wagon reached the base of the hill, his father pulled back on the reins, yelled at the mules, and pressed the brake lever forward with his right foot.

"Get out," he said. "Run for the trees. Hurry."

The boy, with his bow and his few arrows, ran for

37

the cover of the trees and boulders on the hillside, and as he did, he heard the commanding voice of Opothle Yahola ring out over all of the confusion.

"Climb up to the top," he said. "Get up high."

Along with the others, the boy climbed. Near the top of the hill he found himself a snug spot behind a rock about as high as his shoulders. He settled himself in, finding the most comfortable position from which to shoot, and he watched the prairie that spread out before him between the base of the hill and the frozen creek.

In the tense stillness of the waiting, he again heard the voice of the old chief call out an order from somewhere up above.

"Don't waste any shots," Opothle Yahola said. "Wait until your shot is sure."

The wait was not long. He heard the crashing of the horses' hoofs as they entered the icy waters of the creek, and a moment later he saw them emerge into the clearing. The Confederates immediately saw the wagons at the base of the hill, and they charged straight for them. They were about halfway across the prairie when the first shots were fired from the hilltop.

Three soldiers fell from their horses. Two horses fell, throwing their riders. The mass of Confederates continued to charge. A few more fell, but many of them reached the base of the hill and, dismounting, moved on into the cover of the rocks and trees down there.

The boy loosed an arrow and saw it graze the head of a soldier down below. He heard a bullet whiz past his head as he reached for another arrow.

He noticed that the gunshots coming from around him, from the Loyal Creeks, were getting fewer and farther between. That meant that some men had run out of ammunition. He wondered how much longer they would be able to hold out. He himself had but three arrows left.

He looked for another target, but the Confederates who were closest to him were well hidden. He loosed his arrow at a man still on horseback down in the prairie, and he saw the man fall. Then he heard a voice call out above the din, and he thought that it was the voice of Opothle Yahola.

"Fall back. Fall back," the voice cried.

The boy looked to his right and then to his left, and he saw the defenders of the hill turning to run. They ran toward the back side of the hill. They were in full retreat. He wondered where his father and mother and sister were. He looked down the hill and saw Confederate soldiers coming up toward him. They were shrieking their hideous rebel yell. He panicked. He dropped his bow and his last two arrows, and he turned and ran.

He ran across the top of the hill, expecting at any moment to be struck in the back by a bullet. Then he fell, tumbling headlong down the far side. He rolled into a twisted blackjack tree or he might have rolled all the way down to the bottom. He heard the sounds of others running on both sides, and he even occasionally caught a glimpse of someone running past.

He struggled to his feet and started running again down the hill. An outcropping of boulders blocked his path, and he thought he would veer to the right, but a tangle of brush there blocked his way. He ran into the boulders, stopping his motion with the palms of his hands against the rock.

He was just about to move around the rock to his left when the sounds of pursuit behind him startled him. He noticed a niche between the two largest boulders, and he scurried into it like a prairie dog. He tried to hold his breath for fear that the puffs of escaping vapor would betray his hiding place. Occasional shots still sounded, and he heard the noise of people running down the side of the hill. He couldn't see from his hiding place. It might have been Loyal Creeks running away or Confederate soldiers in pursuit.

He lay as quietly as he could, listening to the sounds around him. The rustling of brush, the crunch of footsteps in the snow, shouts and screams and an occasional shot. He heard shouted voices speaking in English, and though he understood very little of it, he was almost sure that they were the voices of Texans.

Eventually the noise died down. It grew quiet. Yet he kept himself still in his hiding place. He did not know how long he remained there in the hole under the big rocks, but he felt the air grow colder. Then he realized that the sun must be low in the western sky. Soon after that it was dark.

He dragged himself out of the hole, and when he stood, his limbs were stiff, and he was shivering from the cold. He moved slowly up the hillside, careful because of the unsure footing, his own stiffness, the dark, and the possibility of the presence of Confederate soldiers.

Once on top of the hill, he could see a line of campfires across the prairie and figured that they must be alongside the frozen creek. It was too far away to see clearly, but he thought that the figures moving around over there must be the Confederates. They had won the day. They had completely routed the Loyal Creeks. The boy wondered about his family. He wondered where they were. He wondered if they were safe and alive.

His shivers had become almost convulsive, and it suddenly occurred to him that he could easily freeze to death. He thought about the wagons down below, abandoned by the Loyal Creeks, and the supplies they contained. In one of those wagons there must be a blanket, he thought.

He made his way painfully down the hill, but the wagons were gone. He looked across the clearing again, but still he could see only the fires dark silhouettes moving about. Now and then he could hear voices drifting across the prairie, but he could not tell what they were saying. Once it sounded to him like laughter.

He heard the crunch of footsteps behind him, and turned quickly to face some unknown danger, but he slipped in the snow and fell, landing heavily on his back.

"Hey, it's okay," a voice said in Creek in a harsh whisper. "Look."

The boy strained his eyes to see in the darkness. There was a form there in front of him, but it was not the size of a man.

"Look. Here on my lapel. My corn-shuck badge."

The boy stood up slowly and stepped toward the

form, squinting his eyes. Then he recognized the dwarf. He had seen him at a distance among the Loyal Creeks with the wagon train, but he had never spoken to the man before and did not even know his name.

"I'm Coka Chupko," said the dwarf. "Are you alone?"

"Yes," said the boy. "Who's over there by the creek? Do you know?"

"It's the Confederates," said Coka Chupko. "They have our wagons and horses and a bunch of prisoners. A few hundred, I think. Men, women, and children. They're celebrating a great victory. But most of our people got away."

"Opothle Yahola?" asked the boy.

"They didn't get him."

The boy wondered again about his family. He wondered if they were among the prisoners or among the dead. He hoped that they had escaped.

"Where are the rest?" he asked. "The ones that got away."

"I don't know," said the dwarf. "You're the first one I've seen. I was captured, but I managed to slip away from them. It's sometimes good to be so small."

The boy shivered convulsively, and the dwarf stepped forward, holding out a blanket. He had another wrapped around his own shoulders.

"Here," he said. "I managed to pick up a couple of blankets on the way out. Put it on."

The boy threw the blanket over his shoulders and pulled it tight around himself.

42

"Mado," he said. "I thought I was going to freeze to death."

"You'll be all right," said Coka Chupko. "Come on. Let's get going."

"Where?" said the boy.

"Oh," said Coka Chupco with a shrug, "I'd say across the hill where the rebels can't see us. I'd say we can build a fire to keep us warm for the night."

"And in the morning, then what do we do?" asked the boy.

"We start walking, I guess."

"Where? What direction?"

"North. To Kansas," said the dwarf. "Where else?"

"But I need to find my family."

"If they're alive, and if they're not prisoners over there, we'll find them in Kansas. Come on now. Let's find a place to build that fire."

The
Green
Peach
War

1880

5

He was now thirty-three years old, and he had a warrior's name in the old Creek tradition. He also had a white man's name, Wilson Jones. That was the name they had put on the rolls. But he didn't use that name. He didn't care for it. His warrior's name, his Creek name, was Chitto Harjo. *Chitto* meant "snake," and it identified him with his clan, the clan of his mother. *Harjo* meant "recklessly brave." He had earned that name as a young boy during the flight to Kansas with Opothle Yahola. Translated into English, his warrior's name became Crazy Snake.

He had a home, a small log cabin, in a clearing at the foot of Tiger Mountain in the Deep Fork District of the Creek Nation. He farmed a little, and he had a dozen good horses. He had a smokehouse, and it was always well supplied with meat. He was not wealthy by white man's standards, or by the standards of the mixed-blood Creeks who were getting more powerful and more influential all the time, but he was doing well enough. He was taking care of his family.

Of course, he did not own the land. No individual Creek could own the land. It was held in common by the Creek Nation for the use of all Creek citizens. He had the use of the land, and he owned the improvements to the land.

He lived in the cabin with his wife, Salina, and their son, Legus. Though he himself did not like to use the English language, he sent his son to school. It was getting more and more difficult to live the old ways, and he wanted Legus to be able to deal with the world and the changes that were coming. He wanted Legus to be able to deal with the white man and not merely be dealt to by him.

The rest of his family, his parents and his sisters, lived in their own homes not far away. They had all come back safely from Kansas at the end of the white man's Civil War, and they had all resettled in the vicinity of Tiger Mountain. It was an easy walk from any one of the homes to any other.

He was thirty-three years old, had his own home, his own wife and son, yet his parents and others of the old ones still called him *chebon*. They would continue to call him "boy" until he was forty years old. That was their way.

At his home he had a small forge at which he made things out of silver. That and sharpening plowshares were his trades, and they brought in a small amount of money. He was working at the forge under an arbor beside his cabin when he saw Coka Chupco coming, driving his small buggy.

He finished what he was doing and laid the work aside as the dwarf pulled back on the reins to stop the pony.

"Climb down, my friend," said Chitto Harjo. "You want some coffee? I think that Salina has some in the house. Almost fresh."

"Yes," said Coka Chupco. "That sounds good to me."

"I'll be right back," said Chitto Harjo. He walked the few steps to his front door and went inside to emerge a moment later with a cup in each hand. As he carried the cups over to the arbor, Salina stepped into the doorway, a broad smile on her face.

"Hello, Salina," said Coka Chupco. "Thanks for the coffee."

"Hello. Are you all right?" said Salina.

"Fine. Thank you."

He took the coffee cup from the hand of Chitto Harjo.

"Will you stay and eat with us?" asked Salina.

"Mado," said the little man. "Yes. I will."

Salina went back inside and shut the door. Chitto Harjo sat in a straight chair under the arbor. He gestured toward another.

"Sit down," he said.

Coka Chupco looked at the chair. There was a wooden keg beside it to serve as a table. He put the coffee cup on the keg, then climbed up into the chair, turned, and sat, his short legs sticking out straight to the front. He picked up the cup and sipped some coffee.

"Ah, that's good," he said. He put the cup back on the keg. "Have you heard the latest news from Okmulgee?"

"I don't know," said Chitto Harjo. "What news are you talking about?"

"Isparhecher's been deposed."

"Deposed?"

"He was a judge, and now he's not a judge anymore. Our new Chief Checote took it away from him."

"Why did he do that?"

Coka Chupco shrugged, picked up his cup, and took another sip.

"I've heard several reasons," he said. "They say that Isparhecher killed a man. It was in his capacity as judge, and the man was a criminal, so it wasn't called murder. But the new chief, they say, thinks that the judge was too zealous in his job."

"I heard about that killing," said Chitto Harjo. "The Lighthorse was not around. Isparhecher did what he had to do. A judge is supposed to uphold law and order. What's he to do if the Lighthorse is not around to do its part of the job?"

"And they say that he's guilty of incest," said the dwarf.

"I don't believe that of Isparhecher. I think that's slander."

"They say that his new wife is his cousin. She's not in his clan," said Coka Chupco. "But they reckon kinship the way the white man does, I guess, and they say that she's his cousin."

Chitto Harjo stood and paced away a few steps, his arms crossed over his chest.

"It sounds to me," he said, "like those are excuses. He ran for office against Checote, and he's claimed that the election was stolen from him with a false count. I think that's the real reason."

"Yes," said the dwarf. "He's the leader of the Loyal Creeks. He's taken the place of Oktarharsas Harjo, and these Pins just want to break his power."

"National constitutionalists, they call themselves," said Chitto Harjo. "They also call themselves progressive."

"Whatever that means," said the dwarf.

Chitto Harjo just muttered.

"They're mostly mixed-bloods," said Coka Chupco, "and they think like white men."

"Yes."

"They act like white men, too, and they want the rest of us to start acting like white men."

"I don't know about them," said Chitto Harjo, "but I'm still a Creek Indian."

"There's going to be a meeting at Nuyaka. Isparhecher called it. Will you be going there?"

"Yes," said Chitto Harjo. "I'll go to the meeting."

They met there at Nuyaka, a small full-blood community built around a ceremonial stomp ground, or square ground. Chitto Harjo and Coka Chupco were there. Isparhecher was there, too, of course, and there was a total of perhaps eight hundred Loyal Creeks in attendance, Chitto Harjo estimated. According to Coka Chupco, 350 of them were "warriors." He counted himself and Chitto Harjo in that number.

People camped out, obviously prepared for an extended stay. There were tents and arbors and lean-tos set up all around the outside edges of the Nuyaka square ground, the ground on which the traditional religious stomp dances were held. In front of the temporary shelters, women cooked over open fires.

Then Isparhecher decided that it was time to address the crowd that was gathered there. An announcement was made, and the people moved into the square ground area. Isparhecher stood behind the altar. He waited for them to settle down and get quiet before he spoke.

"A long time ago," he said, "way back at the beginning, there were no people, no animals living on this world. There was nothing but a dark forest. Then, deep in the middle of the dark forest, Hesaketamese, the Giver of Breath, he made the pine trees start shaking. They shook so hard that pretty soon a cedar tree rocked back and leaned over so far that its roots came up, and out of the hole in the ground, out from under those roots, the people came walking. They came out by clans, and Hesaketamese talked to them then, after they had all come out.

"He told them that the clans were their families, and he told them how to behave. He told them that when they married, they could never marry a member of their own clan. He told them that when they have children, the children belong to their mother's clan. He told them all the things they needed to know in order to live right."

Chitto Harjo had heard all of this before, of course, and he imagined that most of the others gathered there had also heard it. Still, he and the others listened respectfully. It was their chief's way of getting to whatever it was he wanted to tell them. Isparhecher continued.

"But it was cold and it was dark, and the people weren't very happy. They had a hard time finding things to eat, and they shivered in that dark woods. So one day Hesaketamese put a big light up in the sky, and it made the world light. It made it warmer, too, but in case it wasn't warm enough, he sent some hot rocks down from the big light. They were sacred rocks, and Hesaketamese told the people how to use them to make fire. He told them how to get warm by the fires and how to cook their meat. Then he divided day and night and summer and winter. You know all about those stories.

"But Hesaketamese brought those people, our grandfathers, up out of the ground at a special place in a land that he meant for the Creek People. That was our homeland.

"And the white man took it away from us. It was made for us. We came out of that ground, and the white man took it away. We had wars with the white man, and a lot of Creeks got killed. After the wars, they made us sign that treaty and give them all our homeland, and then they made us come out here, and that was a hard journey. Lots of people died along the way.

"But you know, that treaty they made us sign, it

had some good parts in it. It said that after they took away our homelands and gave us this out here in exchange, they would never bother us again. That treaty was forced on us. We didn't ask for it. We didn't want it. It was a no-good treaty for us at the time we signed it. But we did sign it, and we've kept our word ever since then, and the white man should keep his word too."

Then Isparhecher told about the white man's Civil War and how the Creeks had gotten dragged into that, in spite of the efforts of the great leaders of the Loyal Creeks, Oktarharsas Harjo and Opothle Yahola. Then at the end of the war, he said, that white man's war, the United States had forced upon the Creeks yet a new treaty, and with this treaty they took more land, land that they had promised never to touch. This land was then given to the Seminoles, and payment was given to the Creek Nation to be paid out on a per capita basis to all Creek citizens.

But the Loyal Creeks had all refused to accept any of that money because they had not approved of the land sale. Neither did they approve of the mixed-blood Creek government that had agreed to the sale and had signed the treaty with the Confederacy in the first place, leading to all this new trouble.

Isparhecher said that the government of the Creeks was illegal, and that he himself had actually been elected chief. The Loyal Creeks gathered there at Nuyaka all agreed and proclaimed that he was indeed their chief. They said that the new constitution adopted by the Creek Council at their capital,

Okmulgee, was not legal, and they refused to recognize it or to abide by it. Then they proceeded to establish and appoint members to their own Lighthorse police.

Chitto Harjo did not contribute much to these decisions beyond his presence, his agreement, and his vote, but when he and Coka Chupco talked after the meeting had broken up for the day, they agreed with all that had been done.

Then one afternoon, after the meeting had been going on for several days, a man called Sleeping Rabbit came. He talked for a long time to Isparhecher, and then Isparhecher called the meeting to order and introduced the man and let him speak.

"This is Sleeping Rabbit," he said, "and he has come to us from our friends and relatives who live in the Greenleaf Community. They are all Loyal Creeks. He's been telling me things that are very troubling, and now I want him to tell you. Listen to him now."

Sleeping Rabbit told the people gathered there about the trouble between the Greenleaf Creek Community, near the border between the Creek and Cherokee Nations, and their Cherokee neighbors. The trouble had been going on for some time.

Greenleaf Community was populated by full-blood Creeks and Black Creek citizens, freedmen, former slaves of Creek Indians. The Cherokees just across the line were largely mixed-bloods, more white than Cherokee, and the Cherokees had been claiming for some time that the Creeks and Black Creeks, as they called them, from Greenleaf had been sneaking across the line and stealing their horses and cattle. There had been violence before.

Recently, though, Sleeping Rabbit told them, Cherokees had come across the line and taken two of the residents of Greenleaf by force back across into the Cherokee Nation and had hanged them. Creeks had retaliated and there had been a gun battle. Two Cherokees had been killed.

Now Chief Checote was cooperating with the authorities in the Cherokee Nation, trying to apprehend the killers of the Cherokees and punish them. Ten men had been accused, and Sleeping Rabbit said that the men who were accused had not even done the deed.

When Sleeping Rabbit finished his presentation, Isparhecher spoke again. He told the crowd that this was just another example of the incompetence of Checote and further evidence of the new chief's animosity toward the Loyal Creeks. He assured Sleeping Rabbit that he was in sympathy with the residents of Greenleaf Community, and he asked Sleeping Rabbit to tell the people there that if things got too bad for them, they were welcome at Nuyaka, where they would receive the full protection of the Lighthorse of the Loyal Creeks. In the meantime, he asked Sleeping Rabbit to keep him informed of all events at Greenleaf Community. Sleeping Rabbit assured Isparhecher that he would bring him all the news, as well as any messages from that troubled area.

As the meeting continued on for the next several days, more people came in to take part, and they were not all Creeks. Some were Seminoles, and some were Creek freedmen. There was even a band of well-known black horse thieves. Isparhecher made all welcome, for he needed the strength of their numbers.

Then came word that the Creek Nation's Lighthorsemen were on the way to Nuyaka to arrest Isparhecher for treason. That was the final straw.

"Should we overthrow this illegal government?" Isparhecher asked the crowd. "Should we Loyal Creeks take back our own government and save our ancient way of life?"

And the answer from the crowd gathered there at Nuyaka was unanimous.

6

Chief Checote had sent out a posse of Lighthorse police consisting of perhaps twenty men. Riding toward Nuyaka, expecting to make a few arrests, they were astonished when they saw a small army coming toward them. The leader of the posse pulled back the reins of his mount and held up an arm for a halt.

"What the hell is that?" said one of the men.

"They must be Isparhecher's men," said the leader. "Someone warned them we were coming, I guess."

A few shots came from the rambunctious, yelling Loyal Creeks even though the two groups were still too far apart for a good shot.

"Let's get out of here," said the leader of the Creek Nation Lighthorse, and the posse turned to hurry back in the direction from which it had come. The army of Loyal Creeks kept after them for a short distance, then stopped. The one in charge gave some quick instructions, and four men rode on, following the posse to make sure that it kept going. The others turned back toward Nuyaka.

After that brief encounter, Isparhecher ordered guards out constantly to watch for the return of the posse or any other posses that might come out from the Creek Nation, and the people gathered there at Nuyaka evolved into a permanent community. They declared themselves to be the only legitimate government of the Creek People, and Nuyaka their capital.

They further declared the government at Okmulgee to be illegal, and they began making plans for the overthrow of that government. Daily lives took on a routine nature, acquiring and preparing food, washing clothes, watching children. There was constant traffic back and forth from Nuyaka to the homes of those who had moved there. They went back for their cattle or hogs or to tend to their gardens, to harvest and gather the crops in order to take the food back to the settlement.

It was July, a warm day, and Isparhecher and a few others were working on a document they intended to send to Washington, D.C., to protest the old sale of the Creek lands for the use of the Seminoles. None of the Loyal Creeks had ever taken any of the money from that sale.

"We didn't take the money," said Isparhecher. "We didn't sell the land. Those other people, the ones who claim they sold it, they aren't the legal government of this nation. The sale was illegal. It never took place."

A rider came into the camp, dismounted, and hurried over to Isparhecher.

"What is it?" said the chief.

"Two of Checote's Lighthorse just arrested Heneha Chupco," said the man. "They're taking him away right now."

"Take some men and go after him," said Isparhecher. In another few moments thirty Loyal Creek Lighthorse rode out in pursuit of the two arresting officers and their prisoner. They were all well armed.

Sam Scott and Joe Barnett saw the men coming. Scott stopped his horse, and so did Barnett. Heneha Chupco had no choice. He was seated on the back of a horse, his hands tied to the saddle horn. Joe Barnett controlled the horse with a lead rope. Barnett looked at the thirty men coming on toward them fast.

"Sam," he said, "we better get the hell out of here right now."

"No," said Scott. "We can't outrun them. We might as well wait here and face them."

"You could turn me loose," said Heneha Chupco. "Head on home. They won't follow you."

"What do you say, Sam?" said Barnett.

"No way," said Scott. "We have a warrant for this man, and he's going back with us, one way or another."

Heneha Chupco shrugged and smiled.

"There's more than twenty of them," said Barnett. "Maybe thirty."

"We can handle them," said Scott. "Stand firm. They'll back down."

Scott dismounted and stood beside his horse. He had two six-guns in his belt. His rifle was in a saddle boot on the right side of his horse. Barnett was similarly armed. He stayed in the saddle. The riders from Nuyaka pulled up ten feet in front of them and stopped. They were heavily armed and dangerous-looking.

"We want your prisoner," said the leader of the posse of Loyal Creeks. "Turn him loose and you can go in peace."

"And just who the hell are you?" asked Scott.

"Daniel Childers, lieutenant of the Lighthorse, appointed by Isparhecher, Chief of the Creek Nation."

"Daniel Childers?" said Scott. "You the one they call Goob?"

"That's me, all right."

"Well, Goob Childers, I'm Sam Scott, captain of Lighthorse, appointed by Chief Checote, the Principal Chief of the Creek Nation. This is my deputy, Joe Barnett. We're carrying a legal warrant for the arrest of this man. If you interfere, warrants will be issued against you. I suggest that you all just turn around and ride back to New Yorker, or whatever that town is called, and we'll forget the whole thing."

"Your chief is not a legal chief," said Childers, "and you're not legal Lighthorse, so your warrant is no damn good. Leave your prisoner here, and we'll let you ride out."

From his place in the rear of the posse, Chitto Harjo tried to watch and listen. He couldn't see the two lawmen, the captors of Heneha Chupco, very well, and he couldn't hear everything that was being said. All of a sudden he heard a gunshot, then several more. The air was filled with the pungent odor of burnt black powder, and his ears were ringing from the sounds of the explosions. Everyone seemed to be talking at once. He fought to keep his horse under control.

Then, as suddenly, it was quiet again. He backed his horse out of the crowd and rode around to the far right side. He saw them then, Sam Scott and Joe Barnett, lying on the ground, each in his own spreading pool of dark red blood.

Daniel Childers urged his horse forward as he tucked a revolver back into his waistband. Stopping close beside Heneha Chupco, he pulled a knife out from a scabbard at his waist and reached over to cut the rope away from the prisoner's wrists.

"Mado, Goob," said Heneha Chupco.

"Let's go," said Childers.

"Goob," said one of the riders, gesturing toward the bodies, "what about them?"

"Leave them," said Childers, kicking his horse in the sides, "unless you want to take their scalps." As he and the former prisoner rode through the group, the other riders turned to follow. As they made their way back toward Nuyaka, Chitto Harjo thought as he rode, *The next time, they'll send an army.*

It was late July when word reached Isparhecher that an army of constitutional militia had been raised in Okmulgee, the capital of the Creek Nation, by Chief Checote. Under the command of General William Robison, the militia numbered 1,150 men. There were also, according to Isparhecher's sources, several independent volunteer companies in the field.

The Loyal Creeks, including Chitto Harjo, prepared for battle. The Indian doctors or medicine men were kept busy preparing medicine intended to confuse the enemy and to protect the Loyal Creeks. The Loyal Creek soldiers painted their faces for war and pinned corn-shuck badges to their jacket lapels or to their hats. They checked their weapons and counted their ammunition.

Isparhecher, not wanting all of his people to be captured or killed at one place, divided his forces into several small bands and sent them in different directions to watch for the invasion of the constitutional army. Chitto Harjo and Coka Chupco went with a group under the command of Tuckabatchee Harjo, a nephew of the great Opothle

Yahola. They rode toward Okmulgee. Coka Chupco rode atop a small pony in a specially made saddle.

They had not been out long when they saw eight mounted men ahead on a rise. Tuckabatchee Harjo raised a hand and halted his twenty men. The men on the rise had also stopped. For a moment the two groups of mounted men sat in their saddles and studied each other and the situation.

"Who are they, do you think?" asked Coka Chupco.

"They're either constitutionals or volunteers," said Tuckabatchee Harjo. "No one else would be riding toward us armed like that. Let's go get them."

He swept his arm forward and kicked his horse in the sides. As he raced toward the suspected constitutionals, the nineteen other men behind followed him close. Someone fired toward the eight men, a wild shot. The eight turned their horses and retreated down the other side of the rise, disappearing from the view of the Loyal Creeks. The pursuers raced on.

Soon they reached the top of the rise over which the others had vanished, and immediately pulled back on the reins of their mounts. They could see the eight men ahead, but they could also see the larger group, perhaps hundreds, toward which the eight rode.

"They were scouts," said Tuckabatchee Harjo. The eight had turned again, and the hundreds were attacking. Shots sounded, and there was yelling reminiscent of the rebel yells of the white man's

Civil War. One of the Loyal Creeks fell from his horse. The others kept going, running for their lives.

"Scatter out," called Tuckabatchee Harjo. "Every man for himself."

And they scattered.

Having lost the men they were chasing, the constitutional army headed for Pecan Creek, the nearest community that they knew to be sympathetic to the cause of the Loyal Creeks. They found the settlement abandoned. Horses and men all needed a rest, so the officer in charge decided that they would stay there in Pecan Creek for a short while. The men dismounted and allowed the horses to graze. Then one man wandered into the peach orchard behind the houses.

He studied the peaches for a moment, then reached up to pick one. He took a bite, decided that it was good enough, then took another. A couple of other men followed him into the orchard, then a few more. Soon the orchard was full of constitutional soldiers stealing peaches from the Pecan Creek Community orchard.

"One method of attacking the enemy," said a smiling soldier, "is to destroy his food supplies."

"Well," said another, "before we're done here, there won't be many peaches left in this orchard."

"They taste kind of green to me," said a third.

"Aw, they're all right."

Most of the men in the troop were in the orchard eating. Only a few declined. After the captain in charge decided that they had rested long enough, he called for the men to come out of the orchard and get their horses. None came out. He called out again. Still there was no response. He turned to the man beside him.

"Go over there and tell them to get out here," he said.

"Yes, sir," said the other, and he ran toward the orchard. In a few moments, he returned, alone.

"Well?" said the captain. "What's going on? Won't they obey a simple order?"

"Captain," said the other, "they're all sick."

"What?"

"They're all on the ground, rolling over and holding their guts, groaning. Some of them are puking."

"How could they all be sick?"

"It's them peaches, sir. They're too green to eat. And they ate damn near all of them."

The captain stomped away and then stomped back again.

"Go back in there," he said. "Tell them, sick or not, to get to their horses. We're riding out of here. Ask them how they'd like to be caught groaning and puking by some of those wild so-called Loyal Creeks. They're wearing war paint and ready to take scalps. Tell them that."

"Yes, sir," said the other, and he ran back toward the orchard one more time. The captain paced up and down impatiently. There was another man standing nearby, but when the captain spoke again, it was not really to that man. It was more to himself, or to no one in particular. He sort of mumbled. Still, the one standing nearby was able to hear the words.

"We haven't even had a real battle yet," said the captain. "Damn. Just wait. They'll be calling this one the Green Peach War."

7

The constitutional army of the Creek Nation, the all too eager volunteers, and the fifty extra Lighthorsemen added to the force of each district proved to be too much for the Loyal Creeks. The enemy seemed to be everywhere, and the enemy was both better armed and more aggressive than were the followers of Isparhecher. Therefore, after a few minor skirmishes with even fewer serious casualties, the troops of Isparhecher, which, of course, included their women and children, scattered in several directions.

Isparhecher himself and a few of his followers escaped into the safety of the Cherokee Nation. Chief Checote requested that the authorities of the Cherokee Nation arrest the old man for them and send him back into the Creek Nation, but Chief Bushyhead of the Cherokees refused to cooperate.

It was said that his sympathies lay with the full-bloods, not only among the Creeks, but also among his own Cherokee people.

Checote was furious with him and complained bitterly to Agent Tufts, but to no avail. These were internal matters involving the two Indian nations, the federal agent said, and the United States government could not get involved. It was not the policy of the United States, he added, to become involved in the internal affairs of the various Indian tribes or nations.

Checote thought that the United States government had become involved often enough in the past when it seemed to be in its interest to do so, but he kept his thoughts to himself. He was frustrated. He had sympathy for the full-blood traditional Creeks. He understood their point of view, he thought. But he also knew that times were changing, and that they were in danger of being left behind. He did not want to punish the full-bloods, but he could not allow them to continue to advocate armed rebellion.

While Isparhecher and others took advantage of the hospitality of Chief Bushyhead in the Cherokee Nation, some of the Loyal Creeks simply dispersed and went back to their own homes, where they picked up their lives as if nothing had ever happened. Some few of those were later arrested by the Lighthorse or by the volunteer forces or by the constitutional army, all of which continued to roam through the territory occupied by the Loyal Creeks, searching for insurgents. Of those who were arrested, most were chastised, asked to swear allegiance to the government of the Creek Nation, and, having done that, released.

Tuckabatchee Harjo led yet another group, including Chitto Harjo and Coka Chupco, west into the Seminole Nation. It was there that they learned of the fate of Sleeping Rabbit. A runner brought them the news.

"Sleeping Rabbit came back into the Creek Nation," he said. "He said that all he wanted to do was to talk to Agent Tufts about all the problems. He brought some men with him, maybe forty of them. They went to Muskogee to talk with Agent Tufts, and when they got there, soldiers came out and surrounded them right away."

"What kind of soldiers?" asked Coka Chupco.

"Constitutional soldiers, they called them. Creek Nation. They rushed in and surrounded them. Heneha Chupco was there with Sleeping Rabbit, and when the soldiers came, he kicked his horse and started to run away. They shot him down right there in the streets of Muskogee. Shot him in the back while he was running away. Shot him dead. Right in front of a whole bunch of people in the middle of the day. I was there. I saw it happen.

"Then they took Sleeping Rabbit and the others over to Okmulgee and put them in the council house under guard. Nobody saw what happened after that. Only the guards. No one else. But they killed him there. They said that he was trying to run away, and they shot him. *I* think they murdered him. I don't believe that he was trying to escape, but maybe he was. I didn't see it. I don't know for sure."

There was a long silence then before Chitto Harjo spoke. "What about the others," he asked, "the ones who were with him?"

"They made them all sign papers saying that they would be loyal to the Creek Nation from now on. They all signed, I guess, and then were let go. They went on home. That's all."

Not long after that, Isparhecher and the group who had gone to the Cherokee Nation with him came into the Seminole Nation to join those gathered there with Tuckabatchee Harjo. And Isparhecher started making speeches again right away. Things were bad in the Creek Nation, he said. The situation had gotten out of hand. The Loyal Creeks were no match for the forces of the illegal Creek Nation under Chief Checote, that white man's government.

"We need reinforcements," he said. "I'm going west to talk with the Sac and Fox people and with the Comanches. I think I can get them to join us in this fight. What's happened to us will happen to them sooner or later. If I can make them see that, I think they'll join us against the Creek Nation. They're not really Creeks, you know, but a bunch of white men. I'm going to tell those western Indians out there that the United States government will do to them what they've done to us if we don't stop them right now. The U.S. will recognize a bunch of white men as their chiefs, and then they'll use those so-called chiefs to do those tribes in."

The entire group of Loyal Creeks, whole families, wagons, dogs, some Seminoles and some Cherokees, packed up and headed west. They were down to two hundred men and fewer than three hundred women and children, and they were traveling with forty-two wagons. They made it to the Sac and Fox country, and they spent some time there with the Sac and Fox people. Then they went on to the Comanche country. They were no longer in what the U.S. government was calling Indian Territory. They were in the so-called Oklahoma Territory. And the western Indians seemed to be listening to the impassioned message of Isparhecher.

The young clerk opened the door to the office of Agent Tufts in Muskogee, tentatively poking in his head.

"Mr. Tufts?" he said, his voice a question, his manner bordering on frightened.

"What is it?" said the agent curtly, not bothering to look up from his paperwork.

"Chief Checote is here to see you, the chief of the Creeks."

Tufts stood up quickly from his work and glared at the clerk from behind his desk.

"I know who Checote is," he said. "Show him in immediately."

"Yes, sir."

The clerk pushed the door wide open and stepped aside, making a gesture with his arm. "Right in here, Mr., uh, Chief," he said.

Checote walked into the office. Obviously Indian, he was a stout, dignified-looking man, with a neatly trimmed mustache and Vandyke beard. He wore a light gray, three-piece business suit and carried a bowler in his left hand. The clerk stepped out gingerly, shutting the door as quietly as he could. Tufts held out his right hand, and Checote took it in his, giving it a hard grip, the way a white man would.

"Hello, Chief," said Tufts. "It's good to see you. What can I do for you here today?"

"Apparently you can do nothing for me," said Checote. "I've been asking for federal help against these insurgents for some time now and have received none."

"You know that we don't like to interfere with internal matters—" said Tufts. Checote interrupted him.

"I didn't come here to beg or to argue," said the chief. "I just came to inform you. Isparhecher and his followers are said to be on the Comanche reservation. He's trying to arouse the western Indians to join him in an invasion of the Creek Nation in an attempt to overthrow the government.

"Since the United States refuses to live up to its treaty obligations and protect us from domestic disturbances and outside invasion, I'm sending the constitutional army after them into the Comanche reservation."

"Now, wait a minute," said Tufts.

"That's just what I've been doing, Mr. Tufts. Waiting. I cannot afford to wait any longer."

"I understand," said Tufts. "I hesitated to act

73

before, but you're exactly right. This thing has gone too far. I told you that we don't like to interfere in domestic matters, but if they've gone outside of your jurisdiction, then the matter is no longer domestic. I'll request troops immediately from both Fort Gibson and Fort Sill. We'll take care of this problem. Keep your Creek Nation troops inside the Creek Nation. Please. We don't want this thing to get any bigger than it is already. I'll take care of it. I promise you."

On April 23, four troops of United States cavalry under the command of Major J. C. Bates approached the camp of the Loyal Creeks, nine miles east of the Wichita Agency. Isparhecher had received intelligence of the movement of the troops, and the Creeks were ready for battle.

The Loyal Creek warriors were on a hill, braced for the attack. Major Bates sent a messenger with a white flag for a parley. Tuckabatchee Harjo walked out to meet him.

"Major Bates sends his greetings," said the soldier. "He instructed me to tell you that if you surrender peacefully, we will provide you with a safe escort back into the Creek Nation. You will be under our protection. We guarantee your safety."

Tuckabatchee Harjo cocked his head and looked up sideways at the soldier.

"Guarantee, huh?" he said.

"Absolutely. You'll be protected."

"And what will happen then?" asked Tuckabatchee Harjo. "What are you going to do with us when we get back to the Creek Nation? Can you tell me that part?"

"I've only been authorized to tell you what I've just said. We're here to escort you safely back into your own nation."

"What if we don't want to go with you? What if we don't want no escort?"

"My understanding is that we will provide you with such an escort. You will return, one way or another. Why don't you make it the easy way?"

"Well, we'll let you know." Tuckabatchee Harjo turned and walked back toward the defensive line of Loyal Creeks. The soldier watched him for a moment, then turned his mount and rode back toward the troops and the major who waited for him.

From his position on the hill, Chitto Harjo could see the U.S. troops beginning to spread out as if for an attack. He gripped his rifle, ready to shoot. Then he heard the loud commanding voice of Isparhecher.

"Fall back. Fall back. They're going to attack us. Save yourselves. You're on your own."

The Loyal Creek soldiers turned and ran for their wagons and horses. The retreat was completely without order or discipline. The people scattered in all directions. When Major Bates saw what was happening, he shouted frantic orders, and the U.S. troops fanned out even more and hurried forward in an attempt to surround the fugitives.

Chitto Harjo managed to get to a horse, and he pulled Coka Chupco up behind him. They rode west as hard as the horse could go. Looking back over his shoulder, Chitto Harjo saw the circle of blue-suited soldiers closing in on the Creeks who did not manage to escape. He wondered whether Isparhecher had gotten away. He thought for a moment that four soldiers were pursuing him, but he rode on hard. Soon he could see no more pursuit, and he slowed the pace. He did not want to wear out the horse.

"Do you see anyone?" he asked.

"No," said Coka Chupco. "What now? Where are we going to go from here?"

"I don't know. Maybe the Comanche village. We could hide out a day or two, then go back and see if we can find out what happened to the others."

They slept that night in a Comanche tepee, and the next morning they were awakened by the sound of a large number of horses coming into the camp. Coka Chupco was up in a minute, a rifle in his right hand. He ran on short legs to the opening in the tepee. Chitto Harjo was not far behind him. The dwarf stepped outside, and Chitto Harjo ducked low to follow. As he straightened up, he saw his short friend standing still, his rifle still in his right hand but hanging loose by his side. U.S. soldiers were all around them.

Chitto Harjo stood still and looked around. There was a large number of soldiers there, but not so many as those who had first approached the Loyal Creeks where they waited on the hillside. Others must be out rounding up more fugitives, he thought. Then he saw that this bunch already had prisoners.

Surrounded closely by soldiers, Isparhecher and Tuckabatchee Harjo were there, sitting on horseback, their heads down, their hands tied to the saddle horns in front of them.

"You two, put your rifles down easy," said Isparhecher, speaking in the language of the Creeks. "Don't try to resist. Give up quietly. We never planned to fight the whole United States Army."

Chitto Harjo and Coka Chupco carefully laid their rifles on the ground. Then, as two mounted soldiers rode slowly toward them, they raised their hands above their heads. The Green Peach War was over.

The Crazy Snake Rebellion

1900

— 8 —

By the year 1900 the leadership of the Loyal Creeks had passed to Chitto Harjo. He was fifty-three years old, thirteen years past being called "boy." He had been elected to the Creek Nation's House of Kings, one half of the bicameral legislative body of the Creek Nation. He did his best to avoid using the English language, and he did not use his English name.

He had become a prominent citizen of the Creek Nation, respected by the Loyal Creeks and the black freedmen, feared and distrusted by the English-speaking mixed-bloods and whites who lived in the Nation. They knew him as Crazy Snake, and they had begun to refer to his followers, to the Loyal Creeks, as Snakes or Snake Indians.

The Green Peach War, for such it had indeed come to be called, had ended eighteen years previous, but while there had been no threat of further violence or rebellion, all had not been quiet.

In 1882 a group of well-meaning white folks had met in Washington, D.C., and organized the Indian Rights Association. Somehow no Indians had been invited. None had been consulted. The Indian Rights Association dedicated itself to helping the poor Indians by encouraging them along the path to "civilization." If they would not respond to the encouragement, the Association concluded, they would have to be forced. After all, it would be for their own good.

In 1883 the first Lake Mohonk Conference was held in New York State. This would become an annual gathering of do-gooders who, like the members of the Indian Rights Association, thought that they knew best what was best for Indians. Also like the other group, this group did not consider it at all necessary to consult with Indians concerning their welfare. Indians, they thought, were like children. They seldom, if ever, knew what was best for themselves. They had to be guided, and that, more often than not, with a firm hand.

In 1885, at the third Lake Mohonk Conference, Senator Henry Dawes of Massachusetts made a speech in which he proposed that all individual American Indians be made individual landowners and citizens of the United States, like white people. Eventually they would all blend in, and there would be no more Indian problem. There would be no more Indian tribes. In effect, there would be no more Indians. Following a visit to Indian Territory, Dawes described what he had found there, especially in the Cherokee Nation, and he explained the reasoning behind his land allotment theory.

"The head chief told us that there was not a family in that whole nation that had not a home of its own," he said. "There was not a pauper in that nation, and the nation did not owe a dollar. It built its own capitol, in which we had this examination, and it built its schools and its hospitals. Yet the defect of the system was apparent. They have got as far as they can go, because they own their land in common. It is Henry George's system, and under that there is no enterprise to make your home any better than that of your neighbors. There is no selfishness, which is at the bottom of civilization. Till this people will consent to give up their lands, and divide them among their citizens so that each can own the land he cultivates, they will not make much more progress."

Shortly thereafter, Dawes went on to make his proposal in Congress, where it passed. Known as the Dawes Act or the General Allotment Act, it was signed into law on February 8, 1887, by President Grover Cleveland. In 1893 the Dawes Commission was established and charged with the responsibility of carrying out the letter of the law. The Dawes Act itself exempted the so-called Five Civilized Tribes in Indian Territory, but it was soon followed by another act of Congress that targeted them and their lands.

Chitto Harjo and his followers did not believe in the individual ownership of land. The land of the Creek Nation was held in common by and for all of the Creek people. An individual could make use of land, and he could own the improvements on the land. But he could not own the land.

It was a belief basic to everything the traditional Creeks held to be right and true and sacred and solemn. Chitto Harjo and many of his followers attended the big intertribal council that was held at Fort Gibson by the federal government to explain the new law to the Indians. Two thousand people representing twenty-two different tribes were there. Chitto Harjo understood the new law, but he did not like it, and he did not approve of it.

"This is our land," he said. "We did not sell the land. No one has a right to take our land and divide it up for us."

Then he and some other of his followers made a trip to Washington, D.C. They went for copies of the old treaties, which they maintained were sacred, and they hired a lawyer. After listening to their tale, the lawyer told them to go home and establish their own government.

Then, in 1898, the Curtis Act was passed. It all but abolished the five tribal governments in the Indian Territory and forced the allotment process on the tribal members. It called for a final roll to be drawn up of the citizens of each of the five tribes in order to facilitate the allotment process. Chitto Harjo called a council of Loyal Creeks at Hickory Ground near Henryetta. Here they followed the advice of their Washington lawyer.

They declared their sovereignty and proclaimed their intention of living by the old treaties. They would not recognize any newer treaties, they said.

"We did not sign those treaties," said Chitto

Harjo. "They were signed by mixed-bloods who think like white people and who stole our Creek Nation government. We are the Loyal Creeks. We never broke the old treaty. Those Confederate Creeks who call themselves the Creek Nation— they're the ones who broke the treaty. Not us."

Hickory Ground was proclaimed the capital of the new government, and following the earlier example of Isparhecher, Chitto Harjo and the other leaders of the Loyal Creeks appointed their own Lighthorse police. The people gathered there in council, then passed a series of new laws in response to the new troubles that had come upon them.

They made it illegal for Creeks to lease land to a white man or to hire a white man. The punishment for violation of this act was a fine of $100 and fifty lashes. They also passed a law saying that any Creek citizen who received a certificate of allotment for land from the United States government should turn that certificate over to Chitto Harjo.

In the weeks following the council at Hickory Ground, many Creek citizens brought allotment certificates to Chitto Harjo. Some people living in the vicinity of Hickory Grounds were arrested for violating the laws against leasing land to whites or hiring whites. The fines were imposed and they were lashed, according to the law. A general panic spread throughout the Creek Nation.

Then one day U.S. Marshal Leo Bennett rode out to Hickory Grounds to find Chitto Harjo. He looked over the layout carefully. It was his first trip to the place. Hickory Ground was a religous square ground, a place where the ceremonies of the traditional Creek stomp dancers were held.

The ground itself, the cleared area where the dancing took place, was surrounded by four arbors or sheds, one for each of the cardinal directions. To the northeast of the ground was a low mound; to the southeast, another arbor. A little farther out, on all sides, were scattered temporary dwellings.

As Bennett approached the area, he saw that the ground itself was clear, but there were people in the arbors and in and around the temporary dwellings on all sides. As he rode closer, people stood watching him, not quite barring his way. Some held weapons. He rode on, closer to the ceremonial ground itself. Then one man stepped out and stood in front of Bennett. Bennett halted his mount.

"What do you want here?" said the man, speaking English that was not much worse than that used by many of the white intruders into the Creek Nation.

"I'm Leo Bennett, United States marshal."

The Creek man shrugged as if that information meant little or nothing to him.

"What do you want here?" he repeated.

"I want to see Crazy Snake."

"Chitto Harjo is busy right now. I'm Amos Robinson. I'm his official interpreter, so you'll have to talk to me anyhow. Now, what do you want?"

Bennett looked over the stern faces there before him. It would do him no good to try to act tough. He knew that. He heaved a sigh.

"Well, Mr. Robinson," he said, "I have a letter

here from the United States Indian agent for the Creek Indians addressed to Mr. Wilson Jones, also known as Crazy Snake. I was asked by the agent to bring it out here and deliver it personally to Mr. Jones."

"Give me the letter," said the interpreter. "I'll take it to him and read it to him."

Bennett hesitated, but only a moment. The small crowd of dark faces around him had pressed in closer, and it looked to the deputy to be very unfriendly. He reached carefully into an inside coat pocket and withdrew the letter. He handed the letter to Robinson, who took it, glanced at it briefly, then turned and walked away without another word.

Bennett watched nervously as Robinson walked to the arbor that stood on the west side of the square ground. He saw Robinson hand the letter to another man who was sitting there on a bench in the center of the arbor.

That must be the old culprit himself, Bennett thought, *Crazy Snake, Harjo. Damn, these Indians sure do have a lot of names.* He felt a bead of sweat run down the back of his neck and under his collar.

The man Bennett presumed to be Chitto Harjo took the letter from Robinson, glanced at it, and dropped it onto the ground. He glanced in Bennett's direction, then looked away again. Robinson looked toward Bennett, shrugged, turned, and walked off in another direction.

Nervously, cautiously, trying desperately not to let his fear show through, Bennett turned his horse and began to ride away. He noticed that he was holding his breath. A safe distance away at last, he relaxed a little, glad to have gotten out of there with his life, and he resumed his breathing.

Hell, he told himself, *I delivered the damned letter, didn't I? That's all I was told to do.*

It was a few days after that when Coka Chupco saw the soldiers coming. He ran on his short legs for the arbor on the west side of the square ground. Chitto Harjo was there conferring with some others.

"Soldiers are coming," said Coka Chupco.

"What kind?" asked Chitto Harjo.

"United States soldiers."

"How many?"

"I don't know. Too many to fight, and they're too well armed. Besides, they're almost here."

"Then let's see what they want with us," said Chitto Harjo. He stood up and walked toward the road on which the soldiers were approaching. The officer in charge of the troops held up his right arm, and his next in command called a halt of the column. Chitto Harjo, Coka Chupco, Amos Robinson, and a few others walked out to meet them. Chitto Harjo spoke in Creek to his interpreter, Robinson. Then Robinson spoke to the stiff young officer.

"My chief wants to know what you're doing here," he said.

"We've come with a warrant for the arrest of Wilson Jones, also known as Crazy Snake, and for any of his followers we find in his company."

Amos Robinson spoke to Chitto Harjo, who gave him a brief answer. Then Robinson spoke in English again to the soldier.

"That's all of us here," he said.

"Then all of you will go with me to Muskogee under arrest," said the officer. "I hope you'll go quietly in order to avoid any possible bloodshed, but I assure you, you will go."

"We're peaceful people here," said Chitto Harjo, speaking English and startling the army officer. "We'll go along with you."

All of the Loyal Creeks who could be found there in the vicinity of Hickory Grounds were rounded up. They were herded into the road, and the army then surrounded them for the return march to Muskogee. There were eighty-six prisoners. Most of them were full-blood Creeks. Some were black freedmen, who had been slaves of mixed-blood Creeks before the white man's Civil War. A few, like Amos Robinson, were mixed-bloods, Creek and white. No one offered any resistance.

In Muskogee they were lined up against a wall, and a photographer took their picture in a group. They were dressed more or less like the white men of the times, but most of them were wrapped in striped blankets and wore on their heads black hats with wide, flat brims. Crowds of people gathered around to stare.

"I wonder," said Chitto Harjo, "what kind of an animal they think I am."

When the photographer was at last satisfied, the "Snakes" were taken to jail and left there. No one had told them why they had been arrested. No one said how long they would be in jail or what to expect next.

"What are they going to do with us, do you think?" asked Coka Chupco.

Chitto Harjo stared out the small, barred window. Most of the crowd was gone, but a few curious folks still lingered and stared and pointed toward the jail.

"I don't know," he said. "Nothing these people do would surprise me. They might whip us. They might kill us. I don't know."

"We should have fought them," said Coka Chupco.

"It was United States soldiers brought us here," said Chitto Harjo. "Remember? We have a treaty with them."

"Then it seems to me that they've broken the treaty by arresting us and bringing us here."

They stayed locked up for a few days. Then they were taken out of the jail and marched into a courthouse, where a trial was conducted, presided over by a Judge Thomas. Chitto Harjo had never heard of Judge Thomas before, and soon he realized that he was not in a Creek court. He was in a court of the United States.

Chitto Harjo thought that the charges against him and his followers were vague and undefined, but they had something to do with defying the authority of the United States and disobeying the laws of the Creek Nation. As the leader of the group, he was asked to explain himself, and he stood up and spoke with dignity in his own language. Amos Robinson then translated his words into English for the court.

"We have a treaty with the United States," he said, "and we are living by that treaty. We are not defying the authority of the United States. That authority is in that treaty. As far as the laws of the Creek Nation are concerned, that Creek Nation government which the United States is dealing with is not a legal government. We don't recognize it. We are the legal government for the Creek people. And even if that government really were the just and legal government of the Creeks, and if we had broken its laws, then we should be tried in the Creek courts, not in a court of the United States."

He listened carefully for Judge Thomas's response, and it seemed to him that the judge, though he spoke, did not respond to him at all. Instead the judge declared him and all the others to be guilty, and he sentenced them to two years at hard labor in the federal penitentiary at Leavenworth, Kansas. Then he lectured them as if they were so many small and naughty children.

"However," the judge said, "it is my opinion that you did not mean to do wrong. I believe that you simply did not understand the laws and the situation that you find yourselves in. I am not a hard man devoid of feelings. I am in sympathy with your predicament. It is difficult for a simple people to move into an era of enlightened civilization.

"I believe that the justice of the law should be tempered with mercy, when mercy is appropriate, and with that in mind, I have no desire to punish any of you. I only want you to live peacefully under the laws of your own government and of the United States of America, and if I can have your promise of good behavior in the future, I will suspend your sentences. That means, in effect, I will release you without any sentence. You will all be able to go home."

Chitto Harjo stood and spoke in Creek, and he continued standing as Amos Robinson rendered his words into English for the court.

"We are peaceful people," he said. "We always try to conduct ourselves well. We have no intention of raising arms against the Creek Nation or against the United States, and we mean to abide by all just laws."

Apparently satisfied with that response, the judge told them to go home and behave themselves and declared the court to be adjourned.

—— 9 ——

Chitto Harjo continued to tell his followers to refuse to accept their allotment certificates, and he continued to collect, in the name of the Loyal Creek government, the allotment certificates that had been issued to any of his followers. He had not promised the judge that he would stop doing that, nor had he promised to accept an allotment for himself. He had merely promised to be peaceful, and he thought that he had been peaceful all along anyhow. In other words, he thought, he had not promised to do anything any differently than he had been doing all along.

He and the other Loyal Creeks, the Snakes, as others were now calling them, also continued to meet at their own capital, the Hickory Grounds. They started work drawing up their own roll in opposition to the roll of the Creek Nation that was being compiled by the Dawes Commission for purposes of allotment. After all, the white lawyer in Washington had advised them to set up their own government, and that was exactly what they were doing.

But the government of the United States was also moving ahead. Where Chitto Harjo's house stood at the foot of Tiger Mountain, the government agents had drawn lines around him on paper and issued an allotment certificate in his name. And so even though he refused to recognize the validity of the certificate, he was living on what the United States government had determined to be his allotment of land. He was living there with his wife, Salina, their son Legus having by this time established his own home nearby.

The world was changing fast around the Creek people, and Chitto Harjo knew that Legus would be able to deal with the changes, even though he himself was doing all he could to slow them down.

Chitto Harjo lived there on his allotment of land, one mile west of the community of Pierce, sixteen miles from the town of Checotah, but he had sent others, some of his followers, out to tear down the markers that had been put in the ground by the government surveyors to show where the allotments were, and his own certificate was there with all the others he had collected.

It was 1906, and Chitto Harjo was fifty-nine years old. The movement to create the state of Oklahoma out of the combined Oklahoma and Indian Territories was well under way, and, as a final push toward that end, the United States

Congress was considering a bill to bring an end to the tribal governments. Several details of the bill were still being argued, and in an attempt to resolve these arguments, an investigating committee of the United States Senate met in Tulsa—in the Creek Nation. Chitto Harjo and other Loyal Creeks attended the meeting.

Pleasant Porter, Chief of the Creek Nation, was there. He was older, getting gray and rather stout. His demeanor was somber, almost subdued. His hair was cut short in the manner of a white man, and he wore a conservative business suit with a white shirt and tie. He was invited early by the commission to speak. He stood up before the commissioners, Clarence Clark of Wyoming, Chester Long of Kansas, Frank Brandegee of Connecticut, Henry Teller of Colorado, and William Clark of Montana. His expression was grave and troubled.

"I have taken almost every side of this matter," he said, "that anybody else has taken for the past seven or eight years. I've been on all sides of it, and I've been so sure, so often, that I was right, only to come to the conclusion that I was wrong, that I hardly know what to say.

"It was all new to me when it commenced. I did not know anything about allotting lands, excepting that I saw the history of the allotments that were made for the past forty or fifty years, and I saw that each of them proved to be a complete failure.

"I'm satisfied that the government of the United States, from the time of its organization, has tried in good faith to protect the Indians. I have no fault to find. I've made mistakes myself, and I am an Indian.

"I have been for things which I honestly believed were for the good of my race, but that plan, when put in operation, has proved by its results to have been a bad thing. So how could I blame the government for doing things that turned out badly? It's a complex problem, gentlemen. It's something that never was tried before, this trying to educate a people up to a form of government and conditions alien to all their habits of thought and action.

"It's not so much a question of capacity as it is of time. You are the evolution of thousands of years, and we are the evolution of thousands of years. We both probably started at the same point, but our paths diverged. Who can say but that we would finally have reached a stage of civilization toward which we were progressing slowly, but nonetheless surely, which would have suited our life better than the civilization which has been so violently and suddenly thrust upon us?

"I don't know that I have said anything that would suggest remedial legislation, and that, I apprehend, is what you wanted. I have advised so many times in the past and been wrong that I am a little loath to give advice in these days even when it is asked."

Looking very tired and defeated, the old chief sat down. There followed a number of other speakers, and Chitto Harjo gathered that the main topic under consideration was whether the allotted lands should have restrictions placed on them by the government.

The restrictions would be aimed at protecting the new Indian landowners. Since the full-blood Indians were generally considered to be incompetent, as landowners they would not be allowed to sell or lease their own land without first getting permission from the United States government. They would not even be allowed to hold their own land titles. The government would hold the titles for them. He understood that much.

Some speakers argued for that requirement, others argued against it. No one, it seemed to Chitto Harjo, argued about whether the lands should be allotted at all. No one argued about whether there should even be a state of Oklahoma. That, he believed, was what they should be talking about. That was the only real issue at hand. Then at last the commissioners began to call representatives from the traditional factions of the tribes. Eufala Harjo was called.

"We full-blooded Indian people used to live east of the Mississippi River," he said, "and we made a treaty with the white man in 1832. Our Great Ruler was a witness to that treaty."

"Whom do you refer to as the great ruler?" interrupted the chairman, Mr. Clark of Wyoming.

"I mean God," said Eufala Harjo. "God looked upon us all, and he always looks on us and sees us and rules us."

"Well," said Clark, stroking his chin, "go ahead."

"The United States made a treaty," said Eufala Harjo, "and this land was given to us forever, as long as grass should grow and water run. The

United States has divided the land up without the consent of the Indians. We didn't know anything about it until the land was cut up."

"Have you taken your allotment?" asked Senator Long.

Eufala Harjo's answer was strong and emphatic, delivered with no hesitation.

"No," he said.

"Well, what is it you want?" asked the chairman, looking and sounding perplexed.

"I love my treaty," said Eufala Harjo. "I want my treaty back."

"Well, you can't have it back. Can't you understand? It's been modified by other, more recent agreements."

"I cannot take the allotment."

The next speaker called on was Redbird Smith, the leader of the traditional Cherokees. Chitto Harjo was acquainted with Redbird and respected him. He listened carefully as Redbird spoke to the commission.

"I say that I will never change," said the Cherokee. "Before our God, I won't. It extends to heaven, the great treaty that has been made with the government of the United States. Our treaty is respected by God. Our nations and our governments all look to God."

"Congress has provided you," said Chairman Clark, beginning to sound more than a little put out, "a way to make a permanent home. We hope you will agree to the after-treaties that were made."

"I can't stand and live and breathe if I take this allotment," said Redbird. "To take and put the

Indians on the land in severalty would be the same as burying them, for they would not live."

Willis Toby, a Choctaw, said, "They took all our children from their father and their mother and made a guardian for them in the United States court, and we don't want it. I am still faithful to the Great Father who made this treaty, and I am faithful to that treaty and to God."

"I am a full-blood," said Osway Porter, Chickasaw. "I know what the full-bloods want. We never wanted our land divided. I love this country as I love my mother, for it *is* my mother. We want our old original rights to be restored."

And then, at last, as leader of the traditional, full-blood faction of the Creek Nation, Chitto Harjo was invited to speak. He squeezed the hand of Salina, who was seated next to him, then stood up and moved to the front of the room with dignity and pride. His hair, still black, was cut straight just below his ears, and he sported a small mustache. He was dressed in a dark, three-piece suit, white shirt, and black tie. He wore a black hat, which he removed when he went forward to speak. He was accompanied by Amos Robinson, still acting as his interpreter, and when he spoke, he used the Creek language. When he paused, Robinson translated for the commissioners.

"I am telling you now," he said, "about what was done since 1492."

The commissioners looked at one another with expressions both puzzled and exasperated. The chairman, a scowl on his face, turned back toward Amos Robinson.

"All this is unintelligible," the chairman said. "We cannot spend all afternoon in this way. We want you to condense everything. We cannot commence back with the time of the discovery of America. Please translate that to him."

Robinson spoke briefly to Chitto Harjo, and Chitto Harjo nodded his head and began speaking again. When he again paused, Robinson put the new words into English.

"I'm going to make a foundation for what I have to say, for, of course, a thing has to have a root before it can grow. I'm going to talk about 1832 and that treaty."

Several of the commissioners put their heads in their hands. One groaned out loud. Ignoring their rudeness, Chitto Harjo resumed his speech. In another moment, he paused for the interpreter.

"I've always lived back yonder in what is now the state of Alabama. We had our troubles back there, and we had no one to defend us. The troubles were always about taking my country away from me. I could live in peace with all else, but they wanted my country, and I was in trouble defending it."

In spite of themselves, some of the commissioners began to seem to take an interest in what this dignified old man was saying, or at least, in the manner of his presentation. There was something electrifying about his presence, something compelling about his speech. He continued.

"It was no use. Back then it was the government saying to my people, 'Leave your land, the home of your fathers, the land that you love. Look away off

100

to the west, and there you will see a great river called the Mississippi, and away over beyond that is another river called the Arkansas,' and he said, 'You go away out there and you'll find a land that is fair to look on and is fertile, and you go there with your people, and I will give that country to you and your people forever.'"

When Robinson had finished with that, Chitto Harjo still paused a moment to allow it to sink well in. Then he reached inside his coat and withdrew a folded piece of paper, which he held before him in both hands as he spoke further. He still held it while Robinson repeated the next section of his speech.

"That was the agreement and the treaty, and I and my people came out here, and we settled on this land, and I carried out these agreements and treaties in all points and violated none."

The commissioners at this point were visibly nervous. Chairman Clark seemed particularly agitated, but he did not attempt to stop the speech again. Chitto Harjo continued, and his interpreter again spoke the English words.

"This is a copy of the Treaty of 1832, and I do not see anywhere in it any provision for the allotment of our lands. I went to Washington during the winter of last year, and there I spoke to Senator Long. I told Senator Long that I wanted to speak to the President. I told him that if the President told me the treaty provided for allotment, then I would believe it. Senator Long arranged for the interview with the President."

The commissioners looked at one another and raised their eyebrows. Chairman Clark turned back toward Chitto Harjo.

"What did the President say?" he asked.

Chitto Harjo spoke briefly. Amos Robinson looked directly at the chairman and translated.

"He just shook hands with me, and that was all."

His speech was over. He sat down to await a response from the commissioners. There was much discussion. The commissioners talked with one another, and they talked to other government officials who were there. Chitto Harjo did not hear all that was said. He was not particularly interested in what they were saying. He was waiting for a response to his speech. Finally it came from the chairman.

"Mr. Jones," said Clark, "the Treaty of 1832 to which you refer has been modified by subsequent agreements between the Creek Nation and the United States. I hope that you can understand that, and I further hope that you understand that the allotment process is going to go forward. The best thing for you to do is to occupy your own allotment quietly and peacefully. You have a home of your own. There is nothing more to be done."

Chitto Harjo stood up, defiance in his eyes, and he spoke directly to Chairman Clark. He spoke in a loud and clear voice, and he spoke in English.

"I think I have the privilege of appealing to the other tribes," he said, "in response to this disagreement between you and me over this matter of the allotments."

"Do you mean the other four tribes?" asked Clark.

"No. I do not mean the other four civilized tribes. I can call on the Spanish government and the British government and the French government. I can call on civilized governments across the mother of waters to come in and see that this is made right. That is all I have to say."

With that Chitto Harjo turned and walked out of the hall. He was followed by all of the Loyal Creeks and most of the traditional elements of the other tribes represented there. As far as they were concerned, the meeting was over.

10

Oklahoma officially became the forty-sixth state in the Union on November 16, 1907. President Theodore Roosevelt signed the proclamation with a quill plucked from the wing of an Oklahoma eagle. Then a telegram was sent to Guthrie, the temporary capital of the new state, to inform the citizens there that the deed was done.

An immediate shout went up from the throngs gathered there in the new state capital, and it was accompanied by a cacophany of gunshots and exploding fireworks. A temporary stage had been constructed, and a number of dignitaries stood on the platform waiting for the din to settle down. When at last it did, pompous speeches were made, followed by much applause and more shouting and firing of pistols.

Henry Starr, the famous Cherokee bank robber,

was there in the crowd with his wife and infant son. The first governor of the state, Charles N. Haskell, was there, of course. The crowd was made up of both Indians and whites, although the new state constitution did not distinguish between the two.

Then a handsome young white man dressed as a cowboy, but all in white, and a beautiful young Indian woman in all white buckskins stepped onto the platform. A mock marriage ceremony followed, in which the two, symbolizing the Oklahoma Territory and the Indian Territory, respectively, were united to form the state of Oklahoma. Again there was general shouting and applause and shooting of guns.

In the old Deep Fork District of the Creek Nation, now McIntosh County, Oklahoma, there was no such elation. There was no celebration. There was instead gloom, but at the home of Chitto Harjo at the foot of Tiger Mountain, it was a gloom accompanied by a bitter determination to survive, to continue as before, and a stubborn refusal to recognize the authority, even the very existence, of the state of Oklahoma or its county, McIntosh.

Chitto Harjo and his wife, Salina, sat together at a small table inside their cabin. They sat across from each other, and they drank strong black coffee.

"What's going to become of us," she said, "with this new state?"

"I don't know," he said, "but I can't recognize it. I live by the old treaty. I'm not going to try to tell anyone else what to do anymore. They'll all have to make up their own minds. I'll live here quietly. I won't do anything about it, but in my mind I'm the same as always. I'm too old to change."

"What about our son," said Salina, "and his children?"

"It's going to be up to them," he said. "They'll probably go along with the new ways, though. They'll have to, to survive. That's why I want them to get educated in the white man's schools, so they can survive it. Maybe if I had a white man's education, I'd feel differently about it. I don't know. All I know is what I learned at my mother's knees."

The sound of approaching hoofs intruded on their conversation. Chitto Harjo started to get up, but Salina rose to her feet first and put a hand on his shoulder.

"I'll see who it is," she said. She moved to the door and opened it a crack to peek out. Then she opened it wider and spoke over her shoulder to her husband.

"It's Coka Chupco," she said. She stood there waiting while the little man stopped his miniature buggy and jumped down to the ground on his stubby legs. "Come in," she said. "The coffee's still fresh."

"Hello, Salina," said the dwarf. "Is Chitto Harjo at home?"

"Yes. He's home. Come on in."

Coka Chupco stepped in through the door, and Salina shut it again.

"Go on. Sit down there at the table," she said. "I'll get you some coffee."

Coka Chupco climbed up onto the chair that had been occupied by Salina as she moved across the room to get him a cup.

"I just came from Hickory Ground," said Coka Chupco.

"Who's there?" asked Chitto Harjo. "I thought everyone had gone home."

Salina put a coffee cup in front of Coka Chupco. He nodded thanks to her and went on talking.

"Yes," he said. "The Indians went home. There are almost no Indians there. The people there now are nearly all Negroes, freedmen. Old Abe Grayson is there, and they all look to him for leadership. They're living there, all around the ground, in shacks, sheds, lean-tos, and tents. Some got old crates from somewhere, and they're living in those. There are so many of them that the Indians who were there have mostly gone home."

"Abe Grayson's a good man," said Chitto Harjo. "Maybe I should go over there and talk to him and see what's going on."

"Maybe so," said Coka Chupco. He lifted his cup to his lips with his short arm. "I think there might be trouble."

"Why? What kind of trouble?"

Coka Chupco shrugged. "I don't know," he said. "Something from these new state and county people, I think. I don't trust them. The new sheriff of McIntosh County is Dock Odom. You know what he's like. And they say that the new U.S. marshal in Muskogee—What's his name?"

"Arthur Porter?" said Chitto Harjo. "That one?"

"Yes, of course, Porter. How could I forget that

Porter name? They say that he's a cousin of President Roosevelt."

"Yes," said Chitto Harjo. "I heard that too. Well, do you want to ride back over there with me?"

"To Hickory Ground?"

"Yes."

"Sure. I'll go with you. You want to ride in my buggy?"

"Yes. We'll take your buggy."

In Okmulgee, Sheriff Dock Odom stopped in to see the new sheriff of Okmulgee County. W. E. Robertson looked up from his desk a little surprised.

"Dock," he said, "what brings you over here to my county?"

"I've had a whole mess of complaints from citizens, W.E.," said Odom. "They say that the Hickory Grounds are occupied by a bunch of Snakes, and they're afraid of what might happen."

"Oh, yeah," said Robertson. "I've got some of those too. That old stomp ground is over in your county, but it ain't far from some of my communities. People over here are worried too."

"Well, I'm going out there to have a look. I came by here because I thought you might want to ride along with me."

"That's probably a good idea," said Robertson, and he got up and went for his hat.

Chitto Harjo sat with Abe Grayson under the arbor on the west end of the square ground. Each man had a short-stemmed pipe and was smoking.

Soon the pipes were out, and it was time to talk. Grayson had been owned by a Creek during the days of slavery, and he spoke the Creek language fluently.

"Why are the Indians leaving this place?" asked Chitto Harjo.

"They haven't all left," said Grayson. "There are still a few here. But I think that they've been leaving because of Dick Glass."

"The one they say is the leader of a gang of Negro horse thieves?"

"That's the one. I guess the Indians are afraid the law will come out here looking for Dick Glass and his gang. I guess that's why they've been going away from here."

"Why do you stay here, then?" asked Chitto Harjo. "Do you think that you won't be bothered by the new lawmen?"

"I'm worried about them," said Grayson, "but most of my folks here don't have anyplace else to go. I have to think about my people. They look to me, you know. And Dick Glass—well, maybe he does steal a few horses now and then—but he sure gets blamed for a lot of things he didn't do, and he's one of my people too."

Chitto Harjo thought in silence for a moment on the situation that was developing at Hickory Grounds. It was a place of religious worship, but a community, however temporary-looking, had developed around it. It had begun as a Creek traditionalist community. And, of course, there had been a few freedmen among them even then. Now there were only a few Creeks in a predominantly black community. That included the outlaw gang of Dick Glass. Likely the law would be around.

Chitto Harjo thought that the Creeks who had gone back to their homes, who had abandoned Hickory Ground to Abe Grayson and his followers, had probably acted wisely. After all, the loss of Hickory Ground didn't mean so much in the context of the total picture, for it looked as if the full-bloods were about to lose everything.

Chitto Harjo had no ill will for the blacks. Quite a few had been numbered among the Loyal Creeks all along. They had been slaves with Creek Indian owners, and many of them spoke Creek as their first language. Most of them could speak both Creek and English, and in the past, their Creek owners had often used them as go-betweens in their dealings with white men.

The feelings and beliefs and habits of the black freedmen were more closely aligned with those of the Creek full-bloods than with those of the white men or the Creek mixed-bloods, and there had been a significant number of marriages between Creeks and blacks.

The problem at Hickory Ground was not that it was occupied by blacks. The problem was Dick Glass and his outlaws and how the sheriffs of the newly made counties would react to them. Dick Glass, it seemed to Chitto Harjo, was a bigger problem for Abe Grayson than he was for Chitto Harjo.

He was about to speak again to Grayson when he noticed the men of the Hickory Ground community, weapons in hand, band up and move toward the road. He stood and stepped out of the arbor to get a better look. Grayson followed him. They could see in the distance a buggy approaching. Two white men, armed with rifles, were in the buggy.

"Goddamn, Dock," said Robertson. "look at that."

He pulled back on the reins to slow his horse, but he didn't stop. The buggy moved forward slowly, rolling toward the crowd of armed black men who blocked the road.

"They all niggers," said Odom.

They pulled a little closer.

"Not all," said Robertson. "I think I see a couple of Indians."

"How many altogether, you think?"

"I'd say about thirty. What do you want to do now?"

"We can't hardly turn tail and run," said Odom. "They seen us. We got to go ahead on with it."

Robertson heaved a long and heavy sigh. He felt the six-gun at his side. "It's your call," he said, "but if it turns into a fight, we ain't going to win."

"Well," said Odom, "we just have to keep it from going that far. Pull on up there and stop right in front of them."

"What do you want here?" demanded a big man in front of the group in the road. He held a shotgun in his hands.

Dock Odom squinted his eyes, looking off across the square ground toward the western arbor.

"Is that Crazy Snake over there?" he asked.

"What if it is? Who are you?"

"I'm Sheriff Odom of McIntosh County, and this here is Sheriff Robertson of Okmulgee County. We want to talk to Crazy Snake."

No one responded. No one moved.

"We didn't come here for any trouble," said Odom. "Will one of you men tell Crazy Snake we want to talk to him?"

The big man in front looked over his shoulder and said something in Creek, and a younger man turned and ran toward the western arbor. He stopped there for a moment, then ran back. He spoke some Creek words to the big man with the shotgun.

"He don't want to talk to you," said the man.

"Then give him a message from me," said Odom. "Will you do that? Tell him that Sheriff Odom of McIntosh County advises that he break up this meeting and send everyone home. Tell him that."

Again the big man spoke, and again the younger man ran to convey the message to Chitto Harjo. He was back in a moment with the response.

"He said that he don't recognize your authority," said the man with the shotgun. "He don't recognize Oklahoma. He don't recognize McIntosh County. He don't recognize Okmulgee County, and he don't recognize the authority of either one of you. That's your answer."

Odom looked the crowd over. They were angry-looking and stern, and they were well armed.

"All right," he said. "I said what I came to say." He lowered his voice and spoke to Robertson. "Let's get the hell out of here."

* * *

As the buggy moved on away, Coka Chupco spoke to Chitto Harjo.

"They think you're holding a meeting here," he said.

"So it seems," said Chitto Harjo.

"And they came out here looking for you. They don't know what's going on here, do they?"

"Those white men don't know anything," said Chitto Harjo.

It was late in the day, so Chitto Harjo and Coka Chupco spent the night at the Hickory Grounds. They meant to leave in the morning, but before they were ready, the morning brought another white visitor. And this one was accompanied by a squad of U.S. soldiers. Chitto Harjo knew the man in charge. It was Dana Kelsey, the new U.S. agent for the Creek Indians.

"Will you talk to this one?" asked Coka Chupco.

"Yes," said Chitto Harjo. "This man is our agent. He's the man through whom we talk to Washington. We need to try to keep him as a friend. But find an interpreter for me, my friend."

Chitto Harjo met Agent Kelsey with Coka Chupco to his right and a Creek-speaking black man to his left. He spoke through the interpreter to Agent Kelsey.

"Welcome," he said. "We're always glad to see you, but why have you come here today, and why do you have all these soldiers with you?"

"I had a visit yesterday from Sheriff Odom, the new sheriff of McIntosh County," said Kelsey.

"You know that we don't recognize this new state and its new counties," said Chitto Harjo.

"I know that," said Kelsey, "but you're going to have to recognize them. They exist now. It's been done. There's nothing you or anyone else can do to turn things back. You have to learn to live with things the way they are."

Kelsey paused to let his statement soak in. Then he continued.

"I came here today to prevent a fight in which people would get hurt on both sides. Sheriff Odom told me what happened here yesterday. He was ready to put together a posse and come back here prepared to do battle with you. Some of you might have been killed. At the very least, some of you would go to prison. I told him that I thought I could prevent that. I asked him to wait and give me a chance to come out here and talk to you first.

"Will you leave here? Will you go back to your homes?"

"Mr. Kelsey," said Chitto Harjo, "what have we done that we can't be allowed to gather and visit where we want to? Are we less free than the white men? Just because the white men have these new lawmen to speak for them, why are we not allowed to stay here if we want to?"

"The white people around here are afraid that you're planning to cause them some trouble," said Kelsey. "They say that the Snakes are out here making war talk. I don't believe that, but it makes them nervous to know that there are so many of you out here together. Will you go?"

Chitto Harjo looked at his friend Coka Chupco. He thought that he could have told Kelsey that there were almost no Indians, no "Snakes," living at the Hickory Ground anymore, that he and Coka Chupco had just ridden out to see what was happening there, that there had been no "Snake" meeting at all, much less any war talk. He could have explained all that, but he didn't want to give the white man that satisfaction.

"We'll go home," he said. "Tell the new lawmen they don't have to be afraid of the Indians."

Chitto Harjo and Coka Chupco left Hickory Grounds soon after Agent Kelsey's dust had settled in the road. Most of the remaining Creek full-bloods left right after them. The freedmen all stayed behind with one white man and five Creeks. A few of the men stood around in the road watching after the last of the departing Indians as they disappeared down the trail. The big man with the shotgun spoke out loud to anyone who would listen.

"Who do these white folks think they are anyhow?" he said. "Running folks off from their own community. Break up this meeting, they said. What meeting? We live here. Who do they think they are?"

"They got a new state and new laws," said another, "and they're the law. That's who they are."

"This isn't the Creek Nation anymore. It's a white man's state now. It's just like Texas or Arkansas."

"Well, I got me a mind to show them what I think of their new laws and their new state," said the big man. "And I'm going to do it too. Who's going with me? Who's not scared of the white man?"

A dozen men rode out of Hickory Ground. It was almost dark as they headed toward the small town of Henryetta, a distance of only six miles. By the time they reached their destination, it was fully dark, and they approached the town quietly.

"Burn it," shouted the man with the shotgun. "Burn the place down."

They set fire to a store and to one house before anyone in town noticed what was happening. Then men came out of doors with guns, firing at the dark figures in the streets. The dozen arsonists rode away into the dark, laughing, whooping, and hollering, ducking low over their horses' necks. No one was hit. Before they had gotten all the way back home to Hickory Ground, their big leader stopped them.

"Is anyone else here hungry?" he called.

"Yes."

"I'm hungry."

"Has anyone got any meat back at home?" asked the leader.

"No."

"The only meat I've had for three days has been squirrel."

"Squirrel's not meat."

"I got nothing."

"Anyone know where there's a good smokehouse full of real meat?" asked the leader.

"Say . . . yeah! There's a farmer south of here, a white man named Riley. They say he keeps a smokehouse full all the time. Mostly hog meat, they say."

"I could do with a good smoked ham," said the big man. "How about the rest of you?"

They all answered loudly in the affirmative, and he let them yell themselves out before he spoke again.

"Then lead the way to that smokehouse," he said. "We'll have ourselves a feast tonight. That is, unless you're scared of a white man."

"Let's go!" they shouted. "Come on."

They all raced their horses past the big man. He let them go, chuckled to himself, then kicked his horse in the sides and followed them.

Sheriff Odom of McIntosh County was sitting behind his desk in his office in Eufala the next morning. It was late morning, almost noon, and he was thinking about his lunch when the door was flung open and a farmer came stomping in. Odom could tell immediately that something was wrong. The man's face was red with rage.

"Dock," said the farmer, "you got to do something about this. It's your job."

"Sit down, Riley," said Odom, "and tell me what it is I got to do something about."

"Those Snakes," said Riley. "That's what. There's going to be an uprising if you don't put a stop to it right now. In fact, you might say they done rose up."

"What's happened, Riley?"

"Somebody robbed my smokehouse last night. Cleaned me out."

"Did you see who they were?"

"No, I didn't see them, but the smokehouse is empty."

"Then how do you know who did it, Riley?"

"I know. Hell, everybody knows. It was Snake Indians and niggers. Who else would it be? Well, what're you going to do about it?"

"I'll investigate, Riley. I can't go arresting folks without evidence. I'll send my deputy out there soon as he gets back from lunch."

"Deputy, hell. You need to get a whole damn posse together and go out there right now and round them all up," said Riley. "That's what you need to do. Round them up. Or kill them off. One or the other."

"Let me figure out what I need to do, Riley. Hell, you're not the only one with problems. Somebody rode into Henryetta last night and tried to burn the damn town down. I've got that to investigate too. Now, you run along. I said I'll check into it, and I will. Go on. I'll be in touch and let you know what happens. All right?"

"Sheriff?"

"What?" snapped Odom.

"You say someone tried to burn down Henryetta, the whole town?"

"That's right, Riley. That's what I said. They set

119

fire to two buildings before anyone knew what was happening. Then the whole town started shooting at them, but they all got away."

"Did anybody see who it was?" asked the farmer.

"Nobody got a look at any one of them. Same as you and your thieves."

"See?" said Riley. "It was probably them same Snakes that broke into my smokehouse who tried to burn down Henryetta."

"Go home, Riley."

Riley looked as if he wanted to say something more, but instead he turned and stalked out of the office, slamming the door shut behind himself. Odom stood up and paced the floor. In a few minutes Deputy A. Y. Patty came in.

"You eat your lunch?" asked Odom.

"Yeah," said the deputy. He was still sucking his teeth.

"Good. I need you to ride out to Hickory Ground to that Snake camp out there. You know the place?"

"Yeah, I know it. I been there before."

"Well, get on out there, then. Somebody went on a real rampage last night. It's more than those two fires that was set over in Henryetta. Someone emptied old man Riley's smokehouse out. He says it was Snakes. Swears it was Snakes, even though he didn't see them.

"Go on out there and ask some questions. If you can get a look inside any of them shacks or tents out there, take it. Don't try to arrest anyone, though, and don't get in no fights. You got all that?"

"I got it," said Patty. "I'm on the way."

"Be careful," said Odom. "You're investigating, just asking questions. That's all."

"I'll be all right."

Patty rode horseback to the Hickory Grounds. He wore two six-guns and carried a Winchester rifle. He made the trip in good time, riding along at a smart pace, not too fast for the horse, but not dawdling either. When he arrived at Hickory Grounds, he was met in the road by a stern-looking crowd, a big black man with a shotgun standing out in front. Patty sat straight in the saddle, trying to appear unafraid.

"I'm Deputy Patty," he announced. "McIntosh County. I'm here on official business. Now, I don't want no trouble, and I'd appreciate your cooperation."

"What is it you want, Depitty?" said the big man with the shotgun. "You know we don't recognize you or your county out here, don't you?"

"They was arson committed last night," said Patty, ignoring the big man's last question.

"What's that mean?"

"What?" said Patty.

"That word you said. What got committed."

"Oh," said Patty. "Well, it means somebody set some fires in Henryetta—deliberate. They done it on purpose."

"Bad ones?"

"Bad enough. A couple of buildings was pretty near burned up."

"And that's how come you're out here?"

"That's one reason. There was also some theft in the neighborhood."

"You think some of us done it, don't you?"

"The sheriff sent me on out here to ask some questions. That's all. I want to know if anyone here knows anything about any of that."

"No one here knows nothing," said the big man. "How come if anyone does something wrong in the neighborhood, you white folks think right away that we done it?"

Again Patty chose to ignore the big man's question. "Anyone here go into Henryetta last night?" he asked.

"No one left here all night nor all day yesterday. We was all right here the whole damn time. Ever one of us. Ask anyone here."

A chorus of voices backed up the big man. Patty was getting nervous, but he didn't want to crawfish in front of this bunch. It would make the law look weak and ineffective. He didn't think that he could afford to give that impression, so he stood his ground.

"I'd sure like to take a look inside your houses," he said.

"You ain't going to look nowhere," said the big man.

"Ain't you got to have some kind of paper on you before you can do that?" said another voice from the crowd. "Something signed by a judge?"

"If you ain't got nothing to hide, then you shouldn't have no objection to me taking a little look around," said Patty. He started to dismount, but the voice of the big man stopped him.

"You get down off that horse, lawman, and we'll pound your brains into the dirt."

Patty settled back into his saddle and began backing his horse away from the crowd. He kept his hands up high, away from his guns.

"All right," he said. "All right. I'm leaving, but you ain't heard the last of this. I was just asking, but the next one out here will have that paper you asked about, and there'll likely be more men and guns too."

"Then they threatened to kill me," said Patty to Sheriff Robertson of Okmulgee County. "They said they'd pound my brains into the dirt. Well, I got out of there. I mean, I got the hell out of that place as fast as I could without letting them actually see me turn tail and run. Know what I mean? I come over here because it's so much closer than to go all the way back to Eufala."

"You did right," said Robertson. "Damn it. They're not leaving us much choice, are they? I could raise a posse and get right on out there. 'Course, I'd need an okay from Dock."

"Sheriff?" said Patty.

"Yeah?"

"Could I ride with you in that posse?"

"Sure you could," said Robertson. "It's your county, not mine, and Dock did send you out there in the first place. I guess, in a way, you'd really be in charge."

"I'd prefer it if you'd take charge," said Patty.

"All right," said the sheriff. "Just between you and me. But technically it'll be you. Understood?"

"Yes, sir. Understood."

"Then let's get moving," said Robertson. "The day's going to get away from us if we don't hurry along."

When Dock Odom arrived at Robertson's office, following his receipt of a telegraph message, he found a young man in charge.

"Where's the sheriff," he asked, "and my deputy?"

"Who're you?" said the young man.

"I'm Dock Odom, sheriff of McIntosh County."

"Oh. Sure. Yes, sir. Well, sir, the sheriff's gone with a posse out to the Snakes' hangout," said the young man. "Your deputy went with them."

"He did, huh? That's what I was afraid of. How long ago did they leave?"

"Oh, I'd say at least a couple of hours ago. I ain't for sure. Not exactly."

"Damn," said Odom. "There's probably no sense in me trying to catch up with them now. How many men did they take along with them?"

"Let's see," said the youngster, scratching his head. "There was Deputies Ferguson and Chappell, and then there was Mr. Moorey, he's a constable from over at Eufala."

"Yeah," said Odom. "I know him."

"And then there was, uh, nine volunteers went with them, I think." He mouthed names almost silently and counted on his fingers. "Yeah. Nine. There was nine volunteers. One of them was Reverend Fowler."

"A preacher?" asked Odom.

"Yes, sir, but he can shoot. He was raring to go too."

Odom paced the floor. "That's fourteen altogether," he said. "I guess there's nothing for me to do except wait around here and see what happens."

"I guess so, sir," said the young man.

"Damn it," said Odom. "I wish I was with them."

"By God, sir," said the youngster, "me too. I wish I could've gone along with them too. I can shoot as good as anyone else."

The sun was low in the sky, and the posse was still a couple of miles from its destination. Robertson called a halt, then turned his mount to face the men behind him.

"It's going to be dark by the time we get there," he said. "I've been out there before, and they always seem to hear us coming and get ready. I want to surprise them this time. We're going to stop short. When I call a halt next, I want every man to dismount. We're going to surround the camp and wait until morning light. Don't do anything in the morning until you hear me. You got that?"

They rode on in silence until Robertson stopped them again. Then they all dismounted and tied their horses to brush or trees that lined the roadside, and soon they had all faded into the woods to follow the instructions they had been given earlier.

When the sun came up the next morning enough to give light, Robertson surveyed the campsite. A few men and women were moving around in the open. Many had not yet come out of their rude homes. He decided the time was right. He edged around the side of the trunk of a large tree, his rifle in his hands, and he called out.

"You there in the camp. This is Sheriff Robertson of Okmulgee County. Come out in the open with your hands up and no weapons, and no one will get hurt."

There was a moment of confusion. Then those few out in the open ran for cover. Reverend Fowler stepped out from behind a tree, his rifle leveled for action, and someone fired a shot from behind one of the shacks. Fowler screamed in pain and grabbed at his midsection. He leaned forward slowly, then fell backward, landing on his rump. Slowly he tumbled over on his left side, groaning with pain. Another posse member ran to his side. Then, all at once, everyone seemed to start shooting at the same time.

─ 12 ─

Timothy Fowler, the gun-slinging preacher, still lived, groaning and writhing on the ground, blood running freely from his fresh belly wound. His rifle lay on the ground beside him—unfired. The inhabitants of the Hickory Ground shantytown seemed to be firing out of every shack, lean-to, and canvas tent. The members of the posse were equally unrestrained in their shooting. It sounded like one long gunshot, and the air was filled with black smoke and the acrid smell of burning gunpowder.

Robertson wasted three shots, then dropped a black man with a fourth. He was pretty sure from the way the man fell and then did not move that the man was dead. But the fury of the battle caused more than a minor panic inside the sheriff. He looked to his right and called out.

"Patty! Patty, get over here!"

The deputy from McIntosh County ran to Robertson's side.

"What is it, Sheriff?" he said. "You okay?"

"I'm all right," said Robertson, his voice quavering. "There's more of them than I thought. We can't handle it. Send someone to Eufala for help. Hurry."

Patty, crouching low, ran back through the woods until he came to the next member of the posse in line. It was Robertson's deputy, Joe Ferguson.

"Joe," said Patty, "the sheriff wants you to go to Eufala for reinforcements!"

He had to shout to be heard over the din. When Ferguson answered, he, too, shouted.

"Damn good idea!" he yelled. "I'll make it back as fast as I can!"

"Just tell old Dock what we got ourselves into here," hollered Patty, "and be sure and bring along back plenty more ammunition!"

Ferguson ran back through the woods, heading for the place where they had left their horses the night before, and Patty once again turned his attention to the melee at hand. He heard a scream to his right and looked over that way. A posseman had just been hit in the shoulder. He clutched the wound, and blood was running through his fingers, down his arm. Patty thought that he should go to the man's aid, but he didn't know what he'd be able to do. Besides, the battle was still raging. He looked for a target instead.

A lean-to, covered with dry brush, suddenly burst into flames. Patty had no idea what had started the blaze, but he saw a black man come running out of the death trap. Patty fired, and the man dropped, then lay still in front of the flaming hovel, a pool of dark blood widening around him.

Patty wondered what Dock Odom would say when he found out about all this. Dock had sent Patty out to investigate—that was all. Then, after he'd had his life threatened, Patty had gone to the sheriff of the next county and raised a posse, and now they were in a bloody fight to the death. What would Dock say?

He also wondered what time it was getting to be. He wondered where Ferguson was with their reinforcements and ammunition. His own supply of bullets, he noticed, was getting dangerously low, and he was afraid that the other members of the posse were no better off than he.

As if to confirm his thoughts, the firing almost came to a stop. From the nearly constant roar, it changed to a deathly quiet, shattered by an occasional blast. The firing from inside the shantytown slowed in reaction to the now sparse fire from the posse.

The occupants of Hickory Ground were hidden inside their hovels, the members of the posse hidden in brush and behind trees. When Patty could stand it no longer, he crouched low and ran back to where Sheriff Robertson was hiding.

"How long has it been, Sheriff?" he asked. "I mean, since Ferguson left."

Robertson pulled his watch out of his vest pocket and checked it. He tucked it back into place.

"He's been gone about two hours," he said. "How many of them do you think we've hit?"

"I seen two go down and stay," said Patty. "I seen some others get hit and run. I don't know how hard hit they was."

"One of them two dead ones is mine," said Robertson. "I got him right after the shooting started. How's your ammunition holding out?"

"Not so good. I sure hope Ferguson shows up here pretty quick."

"If he don't," said Robertson, "we're whipped."

"Boy," said Patty, "I'd sure hate to have to hightail it out of here."

Abe Grayson huddled in a corner of a small clapboard shack. He had been afraid that he would be killed by bullets passing through the thin walls. He had been afraid that all of his people would be killed in that way. The dwellings at Hickory Ground were far from substantial.

But all of a sudden, most of the shooting seemed to have stopped. Every now and then there was another gunshot, so he knew that the posse was still out there. He wondered why the shooting had slowed down so much. Maybe most of his people were hiding so that the men in the posse didn't have any targets. Or maybe everyone was running out of bullets.

Several shots came then, close together, and at least two of them tore through the walls of the shack in which Grayson hid. Then a man came bursting in through the doorway, diving and rolling on the dirt floor. The shooting ceased again, and the man sat up. He was a young black man, and he held a revolver gripped in his left hand.

"Abe," he said, "you all right?"

"I'm all right, Cholly. How about you? Was all that shooting just now aimed at you?"

Both men were speaking in the Creek language.

"I guess so. I showed myself long enough to run over here to find you. Some of the boys were talking. What are we going to do, Abe?"

"We're going to all get killed," said Grayson, "unless we give it up. That's what we're going to do. We're going to all get killed. Men, women, and children."

"You think we ought to give up?"

"You heard what I said. Give up or get killed. Get everybody killed. I can't say it any plainer than that."

"How do we know they won't kill us anyhow if we try to give ourselves up?"

"I guess we don't know that, boy," said Grayson. "We don't ever know anything for sure, do we? But it's not likely that a sheriff's posse would murder folks after they've given up. We got women and children here among us. We got to think about them too. And so do those lawmen. They got to think about that too."

"Abe," said Cholly, "what do you want me to do?"

"Put that gun down for a start."

Cholly held up the revolver and looked at it for a moment. He heaved a sigh, then put the gun down on the dirt floor of the shack. He looked up at Grayson. The old man glanced around the room, found a dirty white rag and a short stick, tied the rag on one end of the stick, and walked to the doorway. He looked over his shoulder at the younger man.

"You coming with me?" he asked.

"I'm coming, Abe."

Grayson poked the stick out the doorway and waited a moment. No shots were fired. He stuck his arm out a little farther and waited some more. Still no one fired. Slowly, cautiously, he stepped out, holding the white flag up high over his head. Cholly came out behind him.

"Look," said Patty. "Look over there."

"I see them," said Robertson.

"They're giving up."

"Only two of them. That's all I see." Then he raised his voice to call out to the two men under the white flag. "Hold both your hands up high where we can see them, and walk on over this way. Come on."

"Don't shoot," yelled Grayson, using English. "We ain't armed."

"Do what I say," said Robertson, "and no one'll shoot. Keep coming. Right over here. Come on."

Grayson and Cholly, their hands held high, walked across the clearing to the trees and brush where Robertson was concealed.

"Come on," said Robertson. "Come on in here."

"We got women and kids in there, Sheriff," said Grayson.

"Get on back over there. Go on. Right over there. That's right. Now sit down. Both of you."

Grayson and Cholly sat on the ground behind the line of posse men. Robertson and Patty faced them, their guns pointed at their new captives' chests.

"We don't want nobody else to get killed," said Grayson. "We got two dead in there already."

"Three," said Cholly. "And about another dozen wounded, I'd say."

"Is that right?" said Robertson. "Well, we got four out here hurt pretty bad. At least one is like to die. And it's on your heads. You fired the first shot. We'll stop shooting as soon as the rest of them come out just like you did."

"Let me holler out at them, Sheriff," said Grayson. "Maybe I can get them all to come on out."

"Tell them to put their weapons down first. Anyone shows himself with a gun in his hand is liable to get shot."

"I'll tell them."

"All right," said Robertson. "Go ahead, then."

The old man struggled to his feet and, with Robertson watching his every move, walked back to the edge of the woods. He stepped out into the clearing to show himself.

"People," he called out in Creek, "do you hear me in there? Listen to me. You got to quit this fighting. Too many people have been shot and killed already. Put down your guns and step out with your hands up in the air, and no one will get shot. They promised me. I've already given myself up. Cholly's out here with me too. Come on out now, slow and easy. You got to think about the women and children in there. Come on, now."

There followed a long moment of heavy silence. Grayson didn't move. Robertson was still close behind him, his revolver pointed at the old man's back. Then a man peered tentatively out of a canvas tent. Slowly he stepped out, raising his hands. He was followed by a woman and two small children.

"Everyone hold your fire," shouted Robertson. "Hold your fire."

People began to show themselves all around the camp. They came out of every hovel, all holding their hands over their heads. None of them held weapons of any kind. Robertson moved up close behind Grayson.

"Okay," he said, "walk on in there."

He followed Grayson a few steps, then called out again to his posse.

"Move on in, men. Keep them together in a bunch."

As the posse moved in, they pushed the inhabitants of Hickory Ground closer together. Several prisoners were bloody. A few of them moved with difficulty.

"Anyone here any good at doctoring?" Robertson asked Grayson.

"I doctor some," said Grayson, "and Rachel there is pretty good too."

"All right, you two get your wounded over there to the side and tend to them the best you can."

"Yes, sir," said Grayson.

Robertson looked around. "Where's Chappell?" he yelled.

"Right over here, Sheriff," answered the deputy.

"You see what you can do for our wounded. Hurry it up. Patty?"

Patty moved to Robertson's side.

"Yeah?"

"Get a count of these prisoners for me, will you?"

"You bet."

"Sheriff," said another man, "look yonder."

Robertson turned to look toward the road, the direction in which the man had pointed, and he saw Ferguson returning with the reinforcements. Even though the fight was over, the sheriff was glad to see them. He and his posse were far outnumbered by their prisoners, and he had been desperately hoping that the defenders of Hickory Ground would not suddenly somehow become aware of how low on ammunition the posse really was. He was also glad to see a couple of wagons coming along behind the fresh group of men. They would need the wagons for the wounded. Patty came back to his side.

"Sheriff," he said, "I count forty prisoners all told. Five of them is Indian. One's a white man. The rest is all Nigras."

"Just five Indians?" said Robertson.

"Yes, sir. Five."

Robertson walked over to where Grayson was kneeling down beside a man with a shoulder wound. The man was moaning with pain, and Grayson's hands were covered with blood.

"Where's Crazy Snake?" asked the sheriff.

Grayson looked up over his shoulder. "What?" he said.

"I said where's Crazy Snake at?"

"He ain't here," said Grayson.

"He's the leader of this bunch, ain't he?"

"He was here a few days back," said Grayson, "for a visit, but he don't stay here. He's got a home and a farm to take care of. This is just a bunch of folks living here together, Sheriff. These folks kind of look up to me, I guess, but—ain't no leader. Not really."

Robertson strolled back over to where Patty was standing. He stood for a moment stroking his chin. He was a bit more relaxed than he had been just moments earlier, for the reinforcements had dismounted and joined the original posse. They were standing all around the group of prisoners, and the situation was well in hand. But Robertson was more than a bit perplexed.

"Patty," he said, "I ain't exactly sure what we got here."

"What do you mean, Sheriff?" said Patty.

"Well, hell, I thought we came out there to deal with an uprising of Snake Indians. We got forty prisoners here, and only five of them is Indian. And there ain't no Crazy Snake. What the hell is going on here anyhow?"

13

Telegraph and telephone wires were busy over the new state with news of the Crazy Snake Rebellion, which had also already taken on the designation of the Smoked Meat Rebellion. The newspapers reported the arrest of forty Snakes at the Hickory Ground, a ceremonial ground where war dances were held. There was talk of a general Indian uprising led by the bloodthirsty Crazy Snake.

The governor of the new state declared martial law and sent out the militia, and squads of militiamen were seen on all the back roads of McIntosh and Okmulgee Counties, scouring the wooded hills for fugitive Snake Indians. The state soldiers figured out right away that it was very difficult for them to tell a Snake Indian from any other full-blood Indian, so they arrested most of the full-blood Creeks they came across.

Not to be outdone by state officials, Sheriff Dock Odom of McIntosh County requested a warrant for the arrest of Wilson Jones alias Chitto Harjo alias Crazy Snake.

He had an advantage over the militia, he thought, for he knew the location of the home of Crazy Snake. They did not. He also knew what Crazy Snake looked like, and they did not. He knew that they were out rounding up every Indian they could find and leaving it up to the courts to determine whether they were actually Snakes. Then again, Odom thought, most of the full-bloods probably were Snakes, if the truth were told.

But while the militia was running around chasing its own tail and picking up Indians when they ran across them by accident, he would go straight to the source. He would arrest Crazy Snake himself, and he would get the credit. But Dock Odom was in Eufala when the warrant was delivered to his office in Checotah. He hadn't counted on that.

A clerk from the court stepped into the sheriff's office and saw young Herman Odom, the sheriff's son and deputy, sitting behind the desk.

"Hey, Herman," he said, "where's your old man?"

"He's over at Eufala, Bennie," said Herman. "Anything I can do for you?"

"No. I'm just delivering this here warrant. They said he was kind of in a hurry for it."

The clerk dropped the paper on the desk in front of Herman. Herman picked it up and unfolded it to read.

"Oh, yeah," he said. "For old Crazy Snake. Good

deal, Bennie. Dad was in kind of a hurry for this. I think he'd want it served right away too. I'll go ahead and get a posse together."

"Hadn't you ought to wait for him to get back?" asked Bennie.

"Hell, Bennie, I'm a deputy, and he left me in charge of this office while he's out. Ain't no need to wait for him."

Herman Odom rode out of Checotah at the head of a posse of five men. Ed Baum was both a deputy sheriff of McIntosh County and city marshal of Checotah. Frank Jones was a deputy United States marshal. Lee Bateman, Will Carr, and Frank Swift were volunteers from Checotah, deputized by young Odom just for this special duty.

It was the twenty-fifth of March, 1909. They rode to Pierce, a country store just about a mile from the home of Chitto Harjo, and Odom and Jones dismounted and went inside. Mr. Pierce, the proprietor, was behind the counter.

"What'll it be, gents?" asked Pierce.

"We got a posse out here," said Herman Odom. "We got a warrant here for the arrest of Crazy Snake. We know we're about a mile from his house. Just wondered if you'd seen or heard anything that might help us out."

"Well, I ain't seen old Snake for a while," said Pierce, "but I did hear a little something earlier today."

"Like what?" said Jones.

"Fella come in here to buy some flour and coffee. Said he rode by Chotch Harjo's place on the way. Said there was about fifty or sixty Indians gathered up there. Made him nervous, it did. He hurried on by. They just only looked at him, though. He said he was going to take another road on his way back home."

Odom looked at Jones. "What do you think, Frank?" he asked.

"Well, if there's a big gathering of Snakes, it's likely the big Snake will be there, ain't it?"

"I'd say so," said Herman. "Let's go by Chotch's place."

"Let's go."

Chotch Harjo's home was three miles farther than was their original destination and in a slightly different direction. They would not pass the home of Chitto Harjo on the way there, but the news of the big gathering was too much for them to resist. As they approached the house, they saw two Indians in the road ahead. They were walking toward the house. The Indians heard them coming, looked over their shoulders, and started to run.

"Hold it, you two," shouted young Odom.

The two continued to run. Frank Jones pulled his Winchester from its boot, took careful aim, and fired. One of the fleeing Indians pitched forward on his face. The other one stopped running and put his hands over his head. The posse moved forward.

"Don't move," said Jones.

The Indian said something in Creek, but he didn't move. Jones and Herman Odom stopped their horses just behind the man. The rest of the posse pulled up behind them.

"Do you talk English?" said Jones.

The Indian said something again in Creek.

Herman Odom glanced back over his shoulder and looked at Frank Swift.

"Frank," he said, "you stay here and take charge of this prisoner. The rest of you come with me."

He urged his horse forward. Frank Jones rode beside him, and the others followed close, all except Swift. They rode slowly toward the house. They could see no sign of life there.

"Go slow," said Jones. "They could still be in the house. It might be a trap."

The house was a small log cabin. There were no horses or wagons anywhere in sight. The place appeared to be abandoned. Still the posse approached the house with caution. They stopped and dismounted a short distance away, drew their handguns, and ran in a crouch to the house. Jones kicked in the door and jumped inside. Herman Odom moved in right behind him.

"No one here," said Jones. "Damn it."

"If they was here," said Herman, "they're gone now."

"Maybe old Pierce was lying to us," said Jones. "Is he sympathetic to the Snakes' cause?"

"Not that I know of," said Herman. "I never heard of old Pierce to express a political opinion in his life. Maybe they was here. Maybe they heard that we was coming and lit out. Them two outside was headed down here for some reason. I'd say they was coming to the meeting."

"Then likely they didn't get the word that the meeting had moved on," said Jones. "Where would they go from here?"

"Crazy Snake's house?" said Herman with a

shrug. "Where we was headed in the first place. Let's go."

There were ten men in the home of Chitto Harjo. Salina was not at home. There were no women and no children present. The small house seemed crowded with even that number of people. Chitto Harjo sat at the table. To his right, Coka Chupco was perched on a chair. Amos Robinson was there, Washington Riley, Hotgun, the Choctaw Daniel Bell, Lah-tah Micco, Hotulke Fixico, Chotch Harjo, and Legus, son of Chitto Harjo.

Hotulke Fixico was speaking. "We were just talking," he said, "the seven of us, over there at Chotch Harjo's house."

"We were talking about all the recent trouble," said Washington Riley, "and Lah-tah Micco said that we should be talking with Chitto Harjo, so we came over here to see you. We came right away, even though my brother and his son were coming to meet me there at Chotch Harjo's house. They'll wait for me over there, I think. They were just going to walk home with me. That's all. But this talk is important. Maybe they'll come on over here looking for me."

"We came over here because we thought that we should be talking with you about these things," said Amos Robinson to Chitto Harjo. "I'm glad we found you here with your son and with Coka Chupco. But we want to talk about all this trouble."

"They killed people over there at the Hickory Grounds," said Hotulke Fixico. "Lawmen came and surrounded the place and started shooting.

They never shouted a warning. They just started shooting. They killed four men and shot up a bunch of others. There were women and children in there. It was lucky none of them were killed."

"Now they have this new state militia," said Lah-tah Micco. "They're out all over the place riding around. They're rounding up all the Indians they can find, all the full-blood Indians. It doesn't matter who they are or whether or not they've done anything wrong."

"They've even arrested some progressives," said Robinson, and that remark brought a laugh from everyone in the room.

"They say that we've been stealing things and burning houses," said Coka Chupco. "They even say we're making war on the United States. It was the other side that made war on the United States. Those Confederates. We're the Loyal Creeks. We always lived by our treaty with the United States."

"The white man's newspapers are calling it an Indian uprising and Crazy Snake's Rebellion," said Washington Riley. Legus Harjo made a snort at that last remark, but Chitto Harjo still sat quietly, taking it all in, making no comments.

"But it wasn't even any of us Loyal Creeks who did the things they say," said Hotgun. "It was those black freedmen over at the Hickory Grounds. There are no Indians over there anymore."

"Maybe one or two," said Hotulke Fixico.

"It wasn't even all of those black people," said Coka Chupco. "Abe Grayson and his people wouldn't do anything like that. It was probably that Dick Glass gang, those horse thieves."

"But none of that matters to the state militia," said Amos Robinson. "They're still riding around looking for Indians to arrest or kill. What will we do about that? Just wait for them to come and get us?"

Legus, the son of Chitto Harjo, suddenly interrupted the discussion.

"Listen," he said. "Do you hear someone coming?"

He ran to the door and opened it a crack to look out. Out there, coming down the lane toward the house, he saw five riders. He ran back over to the table.

"Five men coming," he said. "White men."

"It's a posse," said Chotch Harjo.

Coka Chupco jumped down off the chair in which he had been sitting. He ran on stubby legs to a corner of the room and grabbed a Winchester rifle almost as long as he was tall. He ran out the door and across the yard toward a rail fence. Reaching the fence, he leveled the rifle across the top rail and fired a shot toward the posse. The shot went over the heads of the riders.

"Scatter," shouted Herman Odom, and the five riders went in different directions, jumping off their horses' backs at different times, each searching for his own secure spot from which to hide and fire.

Ed Baum, six-gun in hand, raced his mount directly toward Coka Chupco. By this time the other Indians were coming out of the house. All of them were armed. Coka Chupco took careful aim and fired again. Baum's head seemed to explode as

144

it jerked back and then fell forward again. His body lurched in the saddle, grew slack, and then toppled off toward the right side to land hard in the dirt with a dull thud. The frightened and confused horse turned first one way, then the other.

"Ed," shouted Herman Odom. He was already off his horse, and he ran on foot toward the fallen Ed Baum. "Ed," he said again. "Son of a bitch."

He dropped to his knees there beside the body, and Coka Chupco fired again. The lead tore through young Odom's sternum. His face registered surprise, not pain, then went blank. He fell forward, across the body of Ed Baum.

"Come on," shouted Chotch Harjo in Creek. "Let's get out of here."

He headed for the woods behind the house, at the foot of Tiger Mountain. The others followed him. Coka Chupco looked around in time to see Chitto Harjo coming out of the house. The others had all reached the edge of the woods.

Just then Frank Jones fired his rifle. Chitto Harjo groaned out loud, faltered, and clutched at his right hip. Coka Chupco fired two wild shots in Jones's direction and ran to the side of the wounded Chitto Harjo.

"Come on," he said. "We'll make it all right."

Posse members fired from their hiding places, and Coka Chupco, walking along beside the limping leader of the Snake Indians, turned occasionally to fire back. Soon they reached the woods at the foot of the mountain.

"Come on, friend," he said, and they crashed

into the thick underbrush. Almost immediately they were climbing. The shock of the shot wore off, and Chitto Harjo began to feel the pain of the wound to his hip. Blood had run down the side of his leg all the way to his foot. It was hot and sticky.

"Leave me," he said. "Save yourself."

"No," said Coka Chupco. "We'll escape together, or they'll catch us both. Come on."

He heard a noise in the brush to his left, and he stepped around, placing himself between his wounded companion and whoever or whatever was approaching. He levered a cartridge into the chamber of his Winchester and held it ready.

"Don't shoot," came a voice in Creek. "It's me, Chotch Harjo."

Coka Chupco lowered the barrel of his rifle.

"Chitto Harjo is hurt," he said. "We have to get him somewhere to safety."

"Follow me," said Chotch Harjo. "I know a place not far where no one will ever find us."

He started climbing up Tiger Mountain. Coka Chupco and Chitto Harjo followed as fast as Chitto Harjo's wound would allow them.

Frank Jones stayed hidden for some time after the shooting had stopped. He looked toward the house and saw no one there. He looked a little to his right and saw the bodies of Ed Baum and Herman Odom lying in the distance. He stepped out a little from his hiding place.

"Men?" he said. No one answered. He called again, a little more loudly. "Men? Can you hear me? This is Frank Jones. Can you hear me out there?"

"I hear you, Frank."

"Who're you?"

"It's me. Lee. Lee Bateman."

"Where's the rest?" called Jones.

"I'm here," yelled Will Carr. "We're it. There ain't no more."

"Well, let's get back to our horses," said Jones. "There's no telling how many of them Snake Indians is still back there in the woods behind that house. Come on. Let's get mounted and get back to poor old Frank Swift. We hadn't ought to have left him alone out there anyhow. Come on."

The three posse members ran after their loose horses, caught them up, and rode fast down the lane away from the home of Chitto Harjo, leaving the bodies of their fallen companions behind.

14

For Chitto Harjo, the climb up Tiger Mountain was a slow and painful one, and the wound to his hip continued to bleed. It needed attention, but the three Creeks had no idea what the posse of white lawmen was doing down below. They could not afford the time, they thought, to stop, wound or no wound. The posse might be in pursuit of them, might even be coming up the mountain right behind them. They had to keep going until they had reached the safety Chotch Harjo had promised them.

It was getting dark. Several times Chitto Harjo faltered and almost fell, but the small man beside him helped to hold up his weight and kept him going. Chitto Harjo's mind flashed back to the time he had first met Coka Chupco. They had been fugitives together then too. Almost fifty years had passed, he realized, and suddenly it was as if nothing had changed at all.

He wondered what would become of his son, Legus, and all the other Loyal Creeks, the traditionalists, the ones the white men were calling Snakes. The others, the mixed-bloods, the progressives, they would all fit in neatly enough. They would be all right. They would find their places in the new state. But he wondered about the full-bloods, the real Indians. And he worried about them.

He did not wonder about himself. He thought that his own life was probably just about over with and finished. He had done all he could with it. He had done his best, and all, it seemed, to no avail. His own fate was not important. He had lived his life, and he had lived it according to what he believed to be right and just and proper. Now he would die.

But what would become of the others? The young ones. Legus and the others.

"It's not far now," he heard Chotch Harjo say. "Only a little ways on up here."

"Hang on, my old friend," said Coka Chupco. "Just a little farther to go."

Just a little farther, thought Chitto Harjo. *Just a little farther. And then what? I've been up this mountain many times, and I've never seen a cave up here. Where are they taking me?*

"Hey," said Coka Chupco. "Where did you go? Chotch Harjo, where are you?"

Some thick bushes seemed to part then right in front of Coka Chupco's face, and there, smiling at him through the brush, was Chotch Harjo, his white teeth shining in the darkness.

"In here. Come on," he said. He reached out, offering a hand to Chitto Harjo, who took it and stepped into the thick brush. Coka Chupco followed, holding a short arm in front of his face to protect it from scratches, and the two soon found themselves with Chotch Harjo inside a dark cave. It was not vast, but there was room to stand and to move around. It seemed, Chitto Harjo thought, about as roomy as his own little house.

Chotch Harjo went to the back of the cave and built a small fire for light.

"Don't worry. No one will see it from outside," he said. "I've checked it all out before. This is a well-hidden place. It's been my secret for a long time now. I knew I was keeping it secret for some good reason."

They helped Chitto Harjo move to the fire and stretch out on his back on the cave floor, getting him as comfortable as they could on the hard, rocky surface. Then Coka Chupco tore the trousers around the wound to expose it for examination.

"Ah, it looks bad, old friend," he said. "I'll try to stop the bleeding, but I don't know what else I'll be able to do."

"While you're doing that," said Chotch Harjo, "I'll go back out and try to find someone to help."

"Look for the woman Fahnee," said Coka Chupco. "She's the best doctor for this kind of thing that I know about."

"Yes. I agree with you. I think I can find her."

Chotch Harjo left the cave without wasting any

more time, and Coka Chupco did his best for the wound while they waited. He took a bandana out of his pocket and cleaned around the wound as well as he could. Then he went outside and felt in the crotches of trees for spiderwebs. When he found some, he took a handful and went back inside the cave, back to the side of Chitto Harjo. He covered the bullet hole with the webs to stop the bleeding.

"My friend," he said, "I'm afraid that will have to do until Chotch Harjo comes back with Fahnee."

"You shouldn't have sent him," said Chitto Harjo. "It's dangerous out there tonight."

"Chotch Harjo will be all right. He can avoid those lawmen. He'll be back here soon with Fahnee, I bet. You rest. I'll go see if I can find some water. You'll be all right here until I get back. I won't be gone long."

"Now, you be careful, too," said Chitto Harjo. "Watch out for those lawmen."

"Ha," said Coka Chupco. "They won't even see me. They have to look down too low to spot me."

He glanced at his rifle leaning against the wall of the cave, but he thought that he would need both hands to carry much water back up the mountain. He left the rifle and went on out the entrance.

Chitto Harjo lay alone in the cave. His whole side hurt from the bullet wound in his hip. It was no longer bleeding, though. He could tell that. Coka Chupco had done that part well. And before long, the little man would be back with water, and then Chotch Harjo would show up with the old medicine woman Fahnee. He guessed that he wouldn't die after all, not just yet.

He smiled wryly, there alone in the cave, to think that he, at his advanced age, was a wounded fugitive. Those white people must think him some kind of wild animal, some monster. Someone had said that the Oklahoma newspapers had headlines that proclaimed that the Snakes were on the warpath.

What had he done? He had kept his faith with the old treaty. He had gone to Washington to talk to the officials there. He had consulted a lawyer. Had he raised a gun or any kind of weapon against a white man? No. He had not. Had he stolen? No. Then what was this warpath?

He wondered where Salina was on this night of violence, and he hoped that his son, Legus, had gotten safely away. He hoped, in fact, that no one else had been hurt.

He knew that it would not end with the events of this night, for he had seen Coka Chupco kill two of the white lawmen. Of course, the lawmen had fired their weapons first, but Chitto Harjo knew that no lawman would consider that simple fact of any real significance.

For a moment he wished that he could have lived in the old days, in the days of Red Eagle, the one the whites had called William Weatherford, the days in which it still made some kind of sense to fight back against the white man. Yet even Red Eagle had failed in the end. He and his so-called Red Sticks had been soundly defeated by the United States Army under the command of the devil Andrew Jackson.

But at least they had fought, and some of them

had killed some white men. What a thing it must have been. What a time to have lived.

But now . . . What would he do now?

Coka Chupco returned carrying a large gourd dipper, dripping water. He also had something slung over his shoulder like a Mexican serape. Chitto Harjo heaved himself up onto one elbow as the dwarf offered him a drink. It was cold and sweet and refreshing.

"Ah," he said. "That's good water. Where did you get it?"

"Right back down at your house," said Coka Chupco. "The same place I got these extra trousers of yours. Those others are messed up."

"You shouldn't have gone there," said Chitto Harjo.

"Why not? There's no one there. No one except two dead white men. The fool lawmen didn't even take the bodies with them. They left their own companions for the coyotes and the buzzards. They don't even act like real human beings."

"Listen," said Chitto Harjo. "I hear someone coming."

Coka Chupco scampered over to the wall of the cave where his rifle stood. He grabbed it and turned to face the entrance, rifle held ready. Then the face of Chotch Harjo appeared.

"There's no need for that," he said. "I told you no one else would ever find this place." He looked back over his shoulder. "Come in," he said.

An old woman followed him inside the cave and moved directly to the side of Chitto Harjo. Daniel Bell the Choctaw came in right behind her.

"Is he all right?" asked Bell.

"I'm all right," said Chitto Harjo, "or at least I will be when Fahnee is through with me."

The old woman put down her basket of herbs and grunted as she examined the wound and the work that had already been done.

"Who did this doctoring?" she asked.

"I did," said Coka Chupco nervously. "I only tried to stop the bleeding."

"Well," she said, "you stopped it. You did all right."

Coka Chupco breathed a sigh of relief and leaned back against the cave wall. Daniel Bell sat down beside him and took out a pipe and a tobacco pouch. He filled the pipe bowl, then lit the tobacco with a faggot from the small fire. After a few puffs, he offered the pipe to Coka Chupco. The little man took it, puffed a few times, and passed it on to Chotch Harjo.

"Is anyone else hurt?" he asked.

"No," said Bell. "I don't think so. I think the other lawmen ran away. They didn't stop for anything."

"They'll be back around in the morning," said Chotch Harjo. "They'll be back, and there will be more of them. They're mad now. They want to get all the Indians."

"All the real Indians," said Coka Chupco.

"No," said Chitto Harjo. "I don't think so."

"What?" said Coka Chupco. "What do you think, then?"

"I think that they want to get Chitto Harjo, the wild animal their minds have created, the leader of the Snake Rebellion. That's what they want. If they think that I'm dead or gone, then I believe they'll quit pretty soon, and I think they'll let the others all go too."

Coka Chupco glanced at Daniel Bell. The Choctaw shrugged. Then there was a long moment of nervous silence while the old woman continued to minister to the wounded Chitto Harjo. Coka Chupco decided finally to break the silence with some small talk. He turned toward Chotch Harjo.

"How did you ever find this place here anyway?" he asked. "I've been up this mountain many times, sometimes alone, sometimes with Chitto Harjo. We've been all over it, and we never knew this place was here. So how did you know about it?"

"Oh, it was maybe twenty years ago, I guess," said Chotch Harjo. "I was out hunting for deer, I think. I'm not sure. It might have been squirrel or rabbits. It was a long time ago. Anyhow, I was up here on this mountain not far from this very spot. That was when I saw the buffalo."

"Buffalo?" said Daniel Bell, incredulous.

"Yes. Buffalo. Big and hairy. There was slobber dripping from his mouth, and he looked right at me and snorted and pawed the ground."

"There are no buffalo around here," said Coka Chupco, "not even twenty years ago. They were all long gone by then."

"It surprised me too. It was the last one, I guess," said Chotch Harjo. "Anyway, it made him mad that I had seen him, and he chased me. I ran, and I fell into the bushes and right on into this cave here. And that's how I found it."

Coka Chupco laughed.

"It's true," said Chotch Harjo.

"And what became of the buffalo?" asked Daniel Bell.

"I don't know," said Chotch Harjo. "I was afraid to come out again. I stayed in here for two days. I never saw the buffalo again. Maybe he went on west to join his brothers, the ones that were left out there. I don't know."

Fahnee sat up straight just then. She heaved a sigh that was half groan and wiped her hands on her long skirt.

"There," she said. "You'll be all right now, but you have to rest here for a few days yet.

"So. You think the white men will keep on bothering us, do you, until they think that you're gone?"

"Yes," said Chitto Harjo. "Until they think that I'm dead or that I've run away somewhere. That's what I believe about them."

"All right then," said the old woman. "When they come back in the morning, I think they'll go right back to your house. Then they'll go to the home of your sister, and they'll look for your wife and son. They'll question all of them if they can find them. So I'll go see them tonight and tell them what to say when the white men come."

She stood up, seemingly with some difficulty, and she turned to face Chotch Harjo.

"At your house tonight," she said, "before they rode on to Chitto Harjo's house, the lawmen killed the brother of Washington Riley. They left his body

156

lying there. Let's you and I go over there and take care of it."

"Now?" said Chotch Harjo.

"Yes," she said. "Right now. Do you have a wagon?"

"No."

"I have a wagon," said Daniel Bell.

"And a team?" said the old woman.

"Yes."

"Then let's go. The three of us."

"What about me?" asked Coka Chupco. "Do you want me to help?"

"Yes. I want you to stay here with Chitto Harjo. I'll be back sometime tomorrow. Don't worry about that."

Without another word, Fahnee ducked her head and walked out of the cave. Daniel Bell and Chotch Harjo, with quick and helpless glances toward Coka Chupco, hurried to follow her out into the darkness.

"What are they going to do, do you think?" asked Coka Chupco.

"I don't know," said Chitto Harjo. "I guess they're going to make a funeral."

— 15 —

Dock Odom was raising a posse in Eufala. Everyone who watched him, those who were volunteering, those being recruited, and those who were simply standing around and observing the activities, marveled at his incredible composure and his stern and businesslike behavior.

They knew that he had just received word that his son had been killed. They knew that Frank Jones had scurried away from the scene of the battle to the nearest telephone and called Dock with the news. And they knew as well that the body was still lying out there unattended, along with that of Ed Baum.

They wondered if Dock had wept, if he had taken time to grieve for the loss of his son. Some thought that he must be awfully hard-hearted. Others simply said that he was one hell of a man. He had a job to do, and he was doing it, even in the face of personal tragedy.

Dock had telephoned Checotah and given instructions for a posse to be raised there. As soon as he got his own bunch together there in Eufala, he had said, he would take them on over to Checotah, where the two posses would be united. Then they would ride out together.

It was already dark when Dock loaded up his posse on the special train commandeered for the purpose and headed for Checotah with them. Along the way he had time to think about what he was doing. There had actually been a gun battle between lawmen and the Snake Indians, and Crazy Snake himself had been there. It was just possible, Dock thought, that this could mean a general uprising of Snake Indians in the area. Perhaps he was taking on too much of the responsibility himself.

When the train arrived at Checotah, and the posse was disembarking to join the others and prepare for their ride out to the home of Crazy Snake, Dock Odom found a telephone in the station and called the governor's mansion.

"I'm not sure," he said, "but there's a lot of unrest in the area. There could be a general uprising of Snake Indians. I think you ought to send out the militia."

Governor Haskell assured Dock that he would do just that. Dock hung up the phone feeling that he had done his duty, but he had no intention of sitting around and waiting for the militia to do its job. He went out into the street to join his posse, and he was pleased to see that, with the Checotah contingent, it had doubled in size.

As he swung into his saddle, one of the men in the posse spoke out.

"Where to, Dock?"

"Crazy Snakes's house," said the sheriff.

Dock Odom did not speak another word as he led the posse toward Tiger Mountain. The word was already out. Everyone knew what they would find out there: the bodies of Ed Baum and Herman Odom. They just hoped, especially for the sheriff's sake, that the bodies would not have been mutilated by Indians or ravaged by scavengers.

The old woman, Fahnee, found Salina Jones, the wife of Chitto Harjo, at the home of her sister-in-law, Polly. Legus was there too. Fahnee spoke first to the young man.

"It's not safe for you here," she said. "You go somewhere to hide."

Then she turned to face the two women, the sister and the wife of Chitto Harjo, the two women she knew the lawmen would search out to question.

"It's been like this for us," said Polly, "since the time we went north with Opothle Yahola."

"I know," said the old woman. "I was there, too, that time. Chitto Harjo is hurt, but I've doctored his wound. He'll be all right. He's hidden away safely for now, and Coka Chupco is with him. Pretty soon now the white men will come back, probably lots of white men. They'll come here looking for you, and they'll ask you where he is.

You say he came by here already. Say he was hurt but not too bad to travel. Tell them that he asked for a blanket, and you gave him one. Then say that he went south. That's all you know. Tell them that."

Daniel Bell and Chotch Harjo were back at the home of Chitto Harjo at the foot of Tiger Mountain. They had Daniel Bell's wagon parked close to the house, and they were inside. They had just laid out the body on the floor, the body of the man who had been killed over near the home of Chotch Harjo. That was what Fahnee had told them to do just before she left them to go do—whatever it was she was going to do. She had not bothered telling them all of her plans. She had warned them, however, not to waste any time.

"Let's get out of here," said Daniel Bell. "The old woman said that we shouldn't hang around too long."

"You're right," said Chotch Harjo. "You take your wagon off somewhere so no one will see it. I'm going back up to the cave."

"Okay. I'll join you up there later—as soon as I can."

Fahnee lived south of Tiger Mountain down on the South Canadian River. From the home of Chitto Harjo, she had gone to the home of Polly and then to her own home. She left a trail that was obvious and easy to follow. And somehow she managed to make it look as if more than one had gone that way. When she reached her home, she went inside the house and built a small fire in the fireplace. She made herself some strong black coffee, poured a cup, and settled back in her rocking chair to wait. She had done all that she could do until they came to her. And she knew they would come.

When the posse reached the home of Chitto Harjo, it was dark. It was late into the night. Actually it was the early morning hours of the next day. There was a bright moon, though, in a clear sky, and because they knew what they were looking for, they all saw the bodies right away.

The posse stopped a short distance back respectfully. As if by prearranged agreement, they would all sit quietly and wait until Dock Odom had visited the body of his son. Dock nudged his mount and rode toward the bodies. Everyone else sat still. The sheriff was still in his saddle when he surprised them all by calling out in a clear, unwavering voice.

"Charlie," he said, "take a lantern and a couple of men and check out the house."

The house was dark and appeared to be deserted.

"Sure, Dock," said the man called Charlie. He rode back to the rear of the posse to the wagon that had followed them along from Checotah. Taking a lantern out of the back, he lit it, adjusted the flame, turned once more, and headed for the house, motioning toward two other men to follow him. They did. They were about halfway to the house when the sheriff spoke again.

"Someone get another lantern lit," he said, "and

come on over here. And bring that wagon along too."

Dock knelt beside the bodies. He hesitated only a moment, then grasped his dead son by the shoulders and pulled the body off that of Baum, laying it out on its back. He took his son's jacket by the lapel and turned it over to expose the inside pocket, and he pulled a folded sheet of paper out of the pocket.

One corner of the paper was blood-soaked, but a glance at it in the dim light showed Dock that it was what he was looking for. It was the warrant for the arrest of Wilson Jones. He folded the jacket back in place and buttoned one button. The wagon rolled up just behind him then, and a man walked up beside it carrying a lantern. Dock stood up, holding the bloody paper in his hand.

"Get out those tarps," he said. "Pick these boys up and load them in the wagon."

He turned away and took a few steps toward the house. Charlie and the other two men were returning.

"Ain't nobody in there, Dock," said Charlie.

"You take a good look?" said Dock.

"The door's standing open," said Charlie. "I just stepped inside and held up the lantern. It's only one room, and there ain't hardly no furniture. I didn't see no one in there."

"It sure looks deserted," said one of the other men who had accompanied Charlie to the house.

"All right," said Dock. "Take this wagon on over to Pierce. You three go along with him."

"Okay, Dock," said Charlie.

The sheriff climbed back onto his horse and rode again to the head of the remaining posse.

"Come on, boys," he said.

It was not far to the home of Legus Harjo, and when the posse got there, they found it, too, deserted. Dock led them on to the home of Polly Jones. There was a light in the house.

"Couple of you boys come on with me," said Dock.

He dismounted, and two others did the same. Dock headed for the door of the small log house, but before he reached it, someone pulled it open from the inside. Dock pulled out a revolver, and his two companions followed his example. An Indian woman stood in the doorway.

"Hello," she said. "What you want here?"

"I'm Dock Odom, sheriff of McIntosh County."

"I know who you are."

"We're looking for Crazy Snake," said Dock. "I've got a warrant here for his arrest." He held the bloody paper out in front of him. "Are you Polly Jones?"

"I'm Polly."

"Wilson Jones, also known as Crazy Snake, is your brother?"

"He's my brother."

"Can I come in and talk to you for a couple of minutes?"

Polly hesitated a moment, then stepped back out of the doorway.

"Come on in," she said.

Dock stepped inside and looked around the room quickly. He saw another woman. No one else.

He put his gun away and turned his head slightly to call out over his shoulder.

"Just stand there at the doorway, boys," he said. He looked back at Polly. "Who's this here with you?" he asked.

"That's Salina," said Polly. "She don't talk English."

"Salina? Is she the wife of Crazy Snake? Is she Mrs. Wilson Jones?"

"Yes," said Polly. "She's my sister-in-law."

"Do you know that Crazy Snake and some other Indians had a fight at his house last evening with a sheriff's posse?" asked Dock.

"Yes," said Polly. "We heard."

"Do you know that two deputies were killed over there?"

"We don't know about that," said Polly. "We was both here."

"Do you know where your brother is right now?"

"No."

Dock nodded his head toward Salina.

"Does she know where her husband is?"

"No. She don't."

"When did you last see your brother?"

"He came by here after the fight," said Polly.

Dock's eyes opened a bit wider.

"He came here? What did he want?"

"He was hurt," said Polly. "Shot right here." She put a hand on her hip. "He was with two other men, and they was going south. He asked me for a blanket, and I gave him one. That's all I know."

"And she was here with you at that time?" asked Dock, again indicating Salina.

165

"Yes," said Polly. "She was here."

"Who were the other two men?"

"Coka Chupco was one," said Polly.

"The dwarf?"

"Yes. The other was Daniel Bell."

"Who's Daniel Bell?"

"He's a Choctaw man," said Polly. "That's who they were. Coka Chupco and Daniel Bell. They left, and they was headed south. That's all we know."

It was not easy trying to read sign in the dark, but with the help of a lantern, Dock tried. He was pretty sure that someone had come straight from Crazy Snake's house to Polly's, and leaving Polly's house, he believed that he could see sign of someone going south.

"Maybe she was telling the truth," he said out loud. "Come on."

They were nearing the South Canadian River when Dock noticed the light in another small log cabin that sat back from the road. He led the posse over to the house, and once again, as they approached, someone inside opened the door. It was an old and bent Indian woman. Dock did not bother to dismount.

"Hello," he said. "You talk English?"

"Yes," she said. "A little."

"Is anyone else in your house?"

"No. Just me. I live here by myself."

"I'm Sheriff Odom of McIntosh County. Dock Odom. What's your name?"

"They call me Fahnee," said the old woman.

"Fahnee," said Dock. "I think I've heard of you. Well, this is a posse I have with me. We're looking for Wilson Jones, also known as Crazy Snake. Do you know him?"

"Everybody knows Chitto Harjo."

"Have you seen him recently?"

"Just a little while ago," said Fahnee. "That's why I'm up so late. Chitto Harjo and two other men stopped here. I fed them a meal, and they went on. Chitto Harjo was hurt in his hip."

"Who were the other two men?" asked Dock.

"A little man," said Fahnee, holding her hand out with the palm down about four feet above the ground. "Coka Chupco. And a Choctaw. His name is Bell, I think."

"Come on, men," said Dock, and he headed back for the road. The faint but unmistakable trail led right on down to the river, and then it disappeared. By this time the sun was peeping above the eastern horizon to light up the early morning sky.

Dock stared at the tracks on the ground, then at the water. It was up and running fast. He looked across toward the far side.

"The tracks stop here," he said. "They crossed the river. Right here."

"Dock," said a rider behind him, "that there river don't look to me like it would be no cinch to cross just now. It's up pretty good."

"Well," said Dock, "the women all told the same story, and the tracks led us right here. You see any sign headed back the other way?"

"No, I sure don't."

"Then they crossed right here," said Dock.

"Well, what are we going to do? We going after them?"

"Nope," said Dock. "A man would have to be crazy or desperate to try to cross that river now, and I'm not either one. Besides, that's Pittsburg County over there. It's out of my jurisdiction. We're going back to Checotah."

Chotch Harjo was panting when he reached the cave near the top of Tiger Mountain. He ducked his head and plowed through the brush and on into the cave. Coka Chupco recognized him and laid aside his rifle. Chitto Harjo was still lying beside the small fire. He was asleep.

—— **16** ——

It was Sunday morning. An unscheduled train pulled into Checotah, and the citizenry, already excited by the activities going on in their neighborhood, clustered around to watch as two companies of state militia disembarked and lined up in their streets. Most of the people gathered there in the street had never seen such a military display, and the excitement level was raised to almost a fever pitch.

One hundred fifty or more armed and uniformed men hurried into formation to the harshly shouted commands of officers, commissioned and noncommissioned. When the ranks were fully formed and the men standing silent and at attention, the growled orders continued.

A tall, mustached man in the most elaborate uniform of all stalked over to a cluster of civilians.

"Where's the sheriff?" he asked.

"He's out with a posse," said one of the men there.

"Who's in charge, then?"

"Well, I don't rightly know," said the other. "All the deputies are in the posse. All but the two that got killed, that is."

"Have you people heard the governor's proclamation?" said the officer.

"We heard something about martial law."

The officer took a piece of paper out of his coat and opened it up to read.

"Upon the telephoned request tonight of Sheriff Odom of McIntosh County, Governor Haskell directed Adjutant General Frank M. Canton to assume charge of the situation, and to order all the necessary militia to the scene of today's battle between the officers and the Creek Indians."

He handed the paper to the man who had been speaking.

"You can post that someplace where everyone can see it," he said. "I'm Frank Canton. Now, can someone here give me directions to the Hickory Grounds?"

Shortly the troops marched out of Checotah, some of the officers on horseback. Frank Canton did not go with them. He placed Colonel Roy Hoffman in charge of the troops in the field. He stayed in town.

"I need to be near a telephone where I can stay in touch with the governor," he said.

Behind his back some of the local residents were talking.

"Did he send them soldier boys out to the Hickory Ground?" asked one.

"That's what he said."

"What the hell for? The fight was at Crazy Snake's house. Over by Pierce."

"Hell, I don't know. I guess the militia knows what it's doing. That's Frank Canton himself. The governor put him in charge of everything. Did you see that suit he's wearing?"

Charlie Coker was half Seminole Indian and half black. He had gotten possession of two revolvers, and he went to find his friend Pudge Warner, another son of former slaves. Both revolvers were loaded, and Coker and Warner felt fully and dangerously armed, even though they had no extra ammunition. They poked the revolvers down the waistbands of their trousers.

"What we going to do now that we got these guns?" asked Warner. "We going to rob somebody?"

"No," said Coker. "'Least, not just yet. I got me something else to do first. You can help me with it if you want to."

"What is it?"

"You know the old woman Fahnee?"

"Yeah," said Warner. "I know her. I don't know her real well, but I know who she is. They say she ain't nobody to mess with."

"That's true enough," said Coker, "but she's a

friend of mine. I seen her this morning, and she give me something to do. She said the laws had been to her house looking for Chitto Harjo. She said the laws are all over the place."

"What's she want you to do?" said Warner.

"She said there's a dead man over to Chitto Harjo's house. Indian man. He's inside the house. She wants me to go over there and set fire to the house."

"Burn Chitto Harjo's house?"

"He ain't going to use it no more. The law's after him. He can't go back home. So Fahnee wants to use the house to finish up the funeral of the man she put in there. That's all."

"We just going over there and set fire to the house?" said Warner.

"That's all," said Coker.

"Well, then," said Warner, "let's go do it."

The day was almost done by the time the two companies of state militia had reached the Hickory Ground and set up their camp. Colonel Hoffman ordered them to pitch their tents in formation. This was to be the headquarters from which they worked.

His second command was to have the shacks and tents that remained standing and everything inside them raked into a pile and burned.

"This filthy place needs a good purging," he said.

While the fire was still burning, sending up billowing clouds of black smoke, he commanded posts to be set in the ground around a substantial area, and wire strung. This enclosed area would be his temporary prison for the Snake Indians he would round up.

When all this was done, the day was over. He had guards posted and sent the rest of the troops to bed.

Dock Odom and his posse did not get back to Checotah until late evening. They had no prisoners, no success to report. They had recovered the two bodies and learned, so they thought, that Crazy Snake, in the company of Coka Chupco and Daniel Bell, had crossed the South Canadian River into Pittsburg County and were headed south. That was all.

Dock went to his office, where he saw the notice Frank Canton had caused to be posted.

"Frank Canton," he said, not quite under his breath. "Huh."

Odom knew about Canton, a gunfighter with a mysterious past. Canton had first achieved notoriety back in 1893 during the famous Johnson County Range War in Wyoming. He had been a detective for the cattlemen's association and was widely believed to have personally murdered several small ranchers and homesteaders.

But before he had taken the job for the stockmen, Canton had been sheriff of Johnson County. He had been elected and supported by the very people he turned against when the cattlemen offered him more money. The small ranchers considered Canton to be a turncoat, a mercenary whose gun was for hire to the highest bidder. And Dock Odom shared their opinion of the man. He knew that he had been the one who called the governor. In spite of that, he resented the presence of Canton in his county, and he told himself that he would not take orders from him. Let Canton and his militia carry on in their own way. Dock Odom still had his blood-soaked warrant. He would continue his own search.

In the office he found a note saying that while he was out, Joe Miller of the famous Miller Brothers 101 Ranch had called. Miller's message was that he had one hundred cowboys ready to be placed at Dock's disposal to fight Indians. "Just say the word."

Dock heaved a heavy sigh and returned Miller's call, using all the tact he could muster to give the big rancher a polite refusal. As he hung up the telephone, he said to himself, "My county's become a damn circus."

Monday morning, Dock put together another posse. This time, though, it was small. He wanted a few carefully chosen men. W. P. Lerblance was half Indian and known far and wide as an expert tracker. Sam Baker had a reputation as a fearless gunfighter and an accurate shot with pistol or rifle. Lee Bateman was a veteran lawman and a cool head.

Dock saw that they were all heavily armed before they rode out of Checotah that morning. They headed straight for the home of Crazy Snake. No one asked Dock why he was going there. He had supposedly made up his mind that Crazy Snake had crossed the South Canadian River into Pittsburg County. Dock didn't bother to tell his small posse why they were going back to Crazy Snake's house. He just led them there, and they followed. He was the boss.

While Dock and his hand-picked posse were riding toward Tiger Mountain, squads of militia rode out in all directions from Hickory Grounds with orders from Colonel Hoffman to round up all "hostile Snake Indians." That was interpreted, for practical reasons, to mean any full-blood Indians found in the vicinity. When any were located, they were arrested and taken back to the Hickory Ground headquarters to be placed in Hoffman's hastily constructed compound, which was being guarded by militiamen.

Charlie Coker and Pudge Warner neared the home of Chitto Harjo. Somewhere along the way, Coker had acquired a two-gallon can of coal oil and some matches. More than once they had ducked into bushes along the roadside when they heard the sounds of approaching horses or foot soldiers and watched as militiamen passed them by.

"The army's come in," Warner had said. "What are they doing here?"

"I don't know," said Coker. "I guess they sure enough think there's a real Indian war going on in these parts."

"Maybe there is," said Warner. "Maybe we just ain't heard about it yet."

"I'm sure glad we got these guns," said Coker.

When they arrived at the cabin at the foot of Tiger Mountain, they paused for a moment. Then they looked at each other.

"Well," said Coker, "let's go on in."

"I don't like to mess with a dead man," said Warner.

"We don't have to touch him," said Coker. "Fahnee already took care of everything. All we have to do is go inside and slop this coal oil around, strike a match to it, and get out of there. That's all."

"Okay," said Warner. "Then let's get to it."

They strode boldly on up to the door, then stopped. They looked at each other again. The door was standing open.

"Come on," said Coker, and he stepped inside. Even though it was daylight, the interior of the cabin was dim, and Coker had to look around before he spotted the body laid out on the floor against the back wall. Its arms were folded neatly across its chest. "There he is," he said.

"Yeah," said Warner, speaking in a harsh whisper as if he were afraid someone might overhear. "Let's get it done."

"Hold on just a minute," said Coker. "Old Crazy Snake's gone. Right? He ain't likely to be coming back here, and even if he does, this place will all be ashes. We might as well take a look around and see if there's anything in here we can use before we burn it all up."

"Well, maybe a quick look," said Warner.

There wasn't much, but what they found, they put in a pile by the door: an iron skillet, a butcher knife, a bolt of calico cloth. They added a few more things to the pile before Coker decided that they should call it quits.

"Carry that stuff on out," he said. "Take it

around back. While you're doing that, I'll be slopping this coal oil around. I don't want to set it off while I'm in here. When I get done, I'll go outside and pitch a match through the window."

"That's a good idea," said Warner, and he started to move the goods they'd scavenged. Coker began to sling coal oil around the room liberally. He still had about half a can when Warner called out to him from the doorway.

"Charlie, someone's coming."

Coker threw down the can and ran for the door. Warner stepped out of the way to keep Coker from running into him, and as Coker ran out, Warner fell in behind him. They ran around the corner of the house just as Dock Odom's posse appeared in the lane.

"It's the law," shouted Warner.

Coker stopped beside the open window and fumbled in his shirt pocket for a match. Pulling one out, he struck it against the side of the house, but it broke. He cursed and threw down the short end, then fumbled for another.

"Hurry up, Charlie," said Warner.

Coker struck the second match and tossed it through the window. It lay on the floor harmlessly, igniting nothing. Nervous and impatient, Warner ran around to the back of the house. He glanced toward the woods as if he'd like to run into them, but he did not. He waited for Coker.

Coker struck a third match and tossed it in close to the can—coal oil was still running out the mouth of the can and puddling. There was a loud poof and a flash, and Coker looked up just in time to see the four lawmen ride into the yard in front of the house. He jerked the revolver from his waistband and ran to join Warner behind the house.

In front of the house the lawmen were dismounting.

"What are we looking for here, Dock?" asked Lee Bateman.

"I don't know, Lee. I just want to look around some in the daylight. Last time I was here it was dark. Let's take a look inside the house."

Bateman was off his horse first, and he walked on up to the door. Just then there was a rush of flame inside. Bateman jumped back.

"The damn place is on fire," he shouted.

Suddenly Charlie Coker made a dash for the woods, and Dock saw him run. He drew out his revolver.

"Hey, you! Stop or I'll shoot!"

Coker stopped, turned, raised his revolver, and fired a shot at Dock.

"Take cover," said Dock, and the four lawmen scattered. Sam Baker ran to the woods to his own right, but he didn't stop there. He moved through the woods toward the back of the house, and he came up even with where Charlie Coker still stood between the house and the woods. Coker fired another shot in the direction of Dock Odom. Baker stepped out of the woods, his revolver aimed at Coker, and Coker either saw him move or heard him. He turned and fired two wild shots in Baker's direction. Baker squeezed the trigger. His one shot dropped Coker. Coker was dead.

Baker walked toward the body. When he was

about halfway, he saw Warner run from behind the house.

"Hold it," he shouted.

Warner ran harder. Baker lifted his revolver, took careful aim, and fired. Warner faltered, ran a few more stumbling steps, then pitched forward. He didn't move.

Baker turned to walk back to where Dock and the others waited, and he saw that the little log house was already engulfed in flames. Soon there would be nothing left.

─── 17 ───

Colonel Roy Hoffman led a squad of mounted militiamen down to the edge of the South Canadian River and called a halt. He had squads of foot soldiers out combing the countryside for full-blood Indians, but he wanted to check this out personally.

According to Dock Odom, the sheriff of McIntosh County, a man highly respected locally, Crazy Snake himself and two other men had crossed the river, escaping into Pittsburg County on their way south to some unknown destination. The sheriff had ended his pursuit at that point.

Well, the state militia's jurisdiction did not stop at county lines, and Hoffman intended to continue the pursuit the sheriff had abandoned.

"Right here is where they say the crossing took place," said the colonel.

"It looks like a dangerous crossing to me, sir," said the sergeant who was riding just to the colonel's left. "The river's up quite a bit, and the current's pretty strong."

"If three old Snake Indians, one of them wounded, could do it," said the colonel, "the Oklahoma State Militia damn well can. Bring the squad and follow me."

"Yes, sir," said the sergeant, and Colonel Hoffman, without looking back, plunged into the turbulent waters. His horse, perhaps showing better sense than its rider, balked and neighed, but the colonel fought him with the reins, kicked him brutally in the sides, raked with his spurs and lashed with his riding quirt.

"Come on," he shouted. "Come on!"

Suddenly the frightened horse began to scream in terror and fight for its own life. It was not going forward, just struggling against something unseen. The colonel shouted and lashed harder at the poor animal with his quirt.

"He's caught up on something, sir," shouted the sergeant.

The horse bucked and screamed, and Colonel Hoffman suddenly went off backward with a yell. For an instant the colonel was out of sight underwater. When his head surfaced, his mouth open and gasping for air, he was several feet downstream.

"Back off, men," ordered the sergeant, and he turned his own mount to ride back up onto dry land. Colonel Hoffman's horse, freed of the burden on its back and of the interfering jerks on its reins, fought itself free of the underwater tangle and trotted up onto the shore.

The sergeant was riding hard alongside the river,

racing the current. He caught up with and rode on past the colonel, who was still being dragged along by the swift waters. Then the sergeant plunged into the water again. Ahead of the colonel, keeping a hold on his reins, the sergeant threw himself off his horse's back and into the colonel's path.

Gasping for air and flailing at the water, Hoffman ran right into his sergeant. The sergeant grabbed the colonel and held him tight with one arm. He still clutched his horse's reins with the other. Then with the help of his horse, he managed to get them all up out of the river. Colonel Hoffman, dripping wet, staggered and coughed and spat. When the coughing at last subsided, he straightened himself up and drew in several deep breaths. Finally he looked directly at his sergeant.

"Bring my horse," he said.

The sergeant called out an order to a corporal, who caught up the horse and led it to where the sergeant and the colonel stood waiting. Hoffman took the reins from the corporal.

"Let's get mounted and head back to camp, Sergeant," he said. "Obviously no one crossed the river here."

The next morning, Dock Odom was sitting behind his desk when the door opened and Frank Canton strode in. Canton swung the door shut behind himself, hardly missing a stride. He stalked over to the sheriff's desk and looked down and across its wide, cluttered surface at Dock, almost glaring.

"I'm General Canton," he said.

Dock looked up as casually as he could manage. He made a quick study of the epaulets and looped braid that falsely broadened the other man's shoulders. He thought that the uniform was certainly gaudy, way out of place for the adjutant general to be wearing out in the field.

"Yeah," he said. "I figured."

"When I arrived in town with my men," Canton said, "you were out with a posse. I guess you left before word of the governor's decree arrived."

"I guess so," said Dock.

"I assume that you've read the proclamation since you got back."

"I read it."

"Then you know that I'm in full charge of this Crazy Snake operation," said the general. "I'll expect to be informed of all your activities from here on—beforehand. No posses are to go out without my prior approval. Is that clear, Sheriff?"

Dock leaned back in his chair and looked Canton in the eye. The man certainly had the look of a paid killer, he thought.

"Mr. Canton," he said, "when you see me in a uniform, you can start giving me orders. Until that time, I'll do my job as I see fit. Is that clear?"

"The governor clearly put me in charge of the whole operation," said Canton.

"Of the military operation," said Dock.

"Read the proclamation, mister," snapped Canton.

"I read it," said Dock. "It doesn't say a damned

thing about civilian authorities, and in spite of the rumors going around, it does not declare martial law."

Canton took a deep breath, trying to control his temper. "I don't know what you're out looking for anyway," he said. "I understand that you believe that Snake escaped across the South Canadian River into Pittsburg County—and out of your jurisdiction."

"The sign indicated that he had done just that," said Dock, "and it was corroborated by the testimony of several witnesses."

"*Snake* witnesses," said Canton. "Completely unreliable, and besides that, there's no way a wounded old man could have crossed that river. My Colonel Hoffman tried it himself last night in an effort to check out your theory, and he was damn near drowned."

"I heard about that," said Dock. "It's too bad the man you've got in charge of your whole field operation can't even sit a saddle."

Canton pointed a trembling finger at Dock's chest, and Dock had the feeling that the famous gunfighter was wishing that he held a six-gun in that hand.

"Now, you listen to me, mister—" Canton began.

"You've said what you came here to say," said Dock, "and I've said all that I intend to on the subject. This conversation's over."

Canton's face burned with outrage, and he stiffened as if snapping to attention. "You just stay out of my way, Sheriff," he said.

"I will, Mr. Canton," said Dock, almost smiling, "and you stay out of mine. We'll get along just fine that way."

Not too far from Hickory Ground, a family of Creek Indians had sat down at their table for their noon meal together. The man, perhaps thirty-five years old, was wearing store-bought clothes, thin from age and wear. The woman, a little younger, wore a long full skirt and a loose-fitting blouse. Her hair was tied up under a red bandana. A teenaged girl and two younger boys completed the family picture.

The woman was about to pour coffee into a cup when the door to their small log cabin was suddenly and violently kicked in. Eight uniformed white men with guns in their hands rushed into the room. The children screamed. The startled woman dropped the coffeepot. The man stood up quickly, knocking his chair over behind himself.

One of the white men shouted something at them, but they could not understand the English words. The man made wild and threatening gestures. The woman said something in Creek, but none of the white men understood her words. The one who seemed to be in charge ignored her. He continued to shout unintelligible words and make wild gestures toward her husband.

The husband spoke, but again there was no understanding. Then the white man spoke sharply to the other white men. Two of them moved around the table, one on each side of the husband. They grabbed him roughly by his arms and led him, practically dragged him, out of the house. The children were crying. The woman was asking desperate questions. The white men took her husband away, his arms tied behind his back.

She and the children ran out of the house and watched as the soldiers marched off down the road. Her husband was surrounded by them. She could see him looking back over his shoulder, his face registering confusion and fear.

Chitto Harjo was standing and walking slowly around in the small cave that had been his home since the day the lawmen had attacked his house. He knew that he no longer had a house. Chotch Harjo had told him about the fire. He walked with deliberate, careful steps and with a slight limp. Over against the wall, Chotch Harjo sat carving a walking stick. Coka Chupco sat near the entryway.

"They say that the state militia has rounded up nearly a hundred Indians," he said. "They have their camp over at Hickory Grounds. It's a military camp now. They have a pen there where they're keeping the Indians they catch. They're keeping them there like cattle."

"And they're not even all Loyal Creeks," said Chotch Harjo. "From what I've heard out there, they have some progressives in that pen too. Anyone who looks like a full-blood Indian gets arrested."

"Full-blood Indian or mixed Indian and black,"

said Coka Chupco. "But not mixed white and Indian."

"Not if the white shows," added Chotch Harjo. He held out the stick he had been carving on. "There. This is done, I think. You want to try it out?"

Chitto Harjo limped over to where Chotch Harjo sat and took the stick in his right hand. He stabbed it at the ground a few times as if testing its strength. Then he leaned on it and took a step. He continued walking around the inside of the cave, poking little holes in the dirt beside his footprints.

"It's good," he said. *"Mado,* my friend. I think I'll be ready to get out of here pretty soon now."

"Not too soon, I hope," said Coka Chupco. "Not while all those state police are running around these parts."

"That shouldn't be too long," said Chotch Harjo. "There can't be very many full-bloods left around here for them to catch.

"So. The cane's all right?"

"Yes," said Chitto Harjo. "It's good."

"How's your wound?" asked Coka Chupco.

"It's doing all right. It's all scabbed over. It hurts a little still, and my hip and leg are stiff, but I can get around. I'll be ready to go—when the militia is gone."

Dock Odom was in a local Checotah eatery having his breakfast when Pierce walked in and headed right for him. Dock was surprised. At first he hadn't even known who Pierce was. He tried to recall, but he believed that this was the first time he had ever seen the man outside of his store, the store that gave the name Pierce to the area out there near the home of Crazy Snake. Pierce reached the table and stopped. Dock nodded a greeting. His mouth was full of food.

"Can I sit down, Dock?"

Dock nodded again, this time toward a chair that was opposite him. He swallowed and picked up a napkin to daub at his mouth while Pierce pulled out the chair and sat.

"They told me I'd find you over here," said Pierce.

"What brings you to town?" asked Dock. "I don't think I've ever seen you in here before."

"I don't come very often," said Pierce, "but I heard something I thought you ought to know."

"Well," said Dock, "what is it?"

"It was a full-blood who told me," said Pierce. "I ain't telling his name. I don't want to get into that. Them folks is my customers, you know."

"That's all right," said Dock. "I don't care who it was. What did he tell you?"

"Well, you know where old Crazy Snake's house used to be?"

"Yeah."

"You know that it's all burned?"

"I watched it burn, Pierce," said Dock. "I was there."

"Oh, yeah. 'Course you was. Well, this full-blood, he told me that there's bones in them ashes.

188

Where the house used to be? There's bones in there."

"Bones?" said Dock. "What kind of bones?"

"Human bones, Dock," said Pierce. "That's what I'm telling you. They's human bones. I wouldn't have come all the way in here to tell you about no dead dog, now, would I?"

— 18 —

Somehow the word spread fast, and when Dock Odom and Lee Bateman rode out of Checotah headed for the allotment of Chitto Harjo, Deputy U.S. Marshal Frank Jones, with a few friends, was not far behind. With a grim look on his face, eating their dust, was Frank Canton, accompanied by his aide. He had sent another militiaman to the Hickory Ground camp with word for Colonel Hoffman to meet him at the home of Crazy Snake.

Dock Odom and Lee Bateman were already examining the bones when Jones and his gang rode up. A small crowd was soon huddled around the pitiful little pile of bones. Canton and his aide came into the yard and dismounted, and Canton pushed his way to the front of the crowd.

"I'm in charge here," he said.

"That's fine with me," said Dock. He stood up and started walking toward his horse. Bateman followed him. One of Jones's companions squinted down at the grim relics.

"Them's human bones, all right, I'd say," he said.

Canton turned toward Dock and spoke in a loud voice. "Hold on," he said.

Dock stopped beside his horse and turned to face the elaborately dressed head of the state militia. He thought, *the bastard looks like he's going to a fancy dress ball or something.*

"What do you say now, Dock?" asked Canton.

"About what?"

"About this," said Canton, gesturing toward the bones. "You still think Crazy Snake got across the river? You still think he's alive and moving south?"

"I haven't seen anything to change my mind," said Dock.

"What about these bones here?"

"Sorry," said Dock. "I don't recognize them."

"There was a gunfight here," said Canton. "Crazy Snake was here during the fight. He was shot. This ash heap is what's left of his house, and I say that them there is his bones. He's dead."

Frank Jones then stepped forward.

"Well, General," he said, "I ain't so sure about that. I was here. I took part in that fight, you know. You're right that old Snake was here, and he got shot. You're right about that. But I seen him run away into the woods. I don't rightly see how that could be him."

Dock put a foot in a stirrup and swung himself up onto the back of his horse. "Crazy Snake's somewhere south of the Canadian River," he said.

"I talked to three witnesses who saw him along the way."

"Snake Indians," snapped Canton.

"They knew he was wounded," said Dock. "Knew where he was shot. They also knew who was traveling with him. Their stories all matched. He's gone, Mr. Canton."

Dock emphasized the word *mister,* as if to underscore the fact that he was not using Canton's proper title. It was a deliberate insult. He knew it, and he hoped that Canton recognized it for what it was.

"Even if your witnesses were telling the truth," said Canton, "Snake likely got to the river and found out that he couldn't cross it. He probably came back here then."

A whole squad of mounted and uniformed men rode up just then. Colonel Roy Hoffman was in the lead. He called a halt to the squad, got down off his horse, leaving the others mounted, and walked toward Canton, giving a snappy salute. Dock turned his own mount and kicked it in the sides. Bateman followed his example.

"Hey," shouted Canton, "where the hell do you think you're going?"

Dock kept riding, but he did turn his head slightly to call back to Canton. "You're in charge here," he said. "I'm going home."

In a few more days the neighborhoods around both the Hickory Ground and Tiger Mountain had quieted considerably. Word was out that Roy Hoffman had rounded up eighty-six "Snake Indians." Sheriff's posses and deputy U.S. marshals had detained another sixty-six, bringing the total up to over 150. Colonel Hoffman, at the orders of Adjutant General Canton, marched the prisoners into Muskogee to turn them over to the federal court there. Its job over, the militia left. The argument over the bones discovered in the ashes at the home of Chitto Harjo was never resolved.

Dock Odom and several others wired or telephoned complaints to the governor's office about the way in which Frank Canton had conducted the operations of the state militia, so the governor sent the famous lawman Bill Tilghman to investigate. Nothing ever came of the investigation.

Late one night, Chitto Harjo, Coka Chupco, and Chotch Harjo came out of the cave and descended Tiger Mountain. Near the ash pile that had been Chitto Harjo's house, Daniel Bell waited with his wagon. In the wagon were blankets and food. The three Loyal Creeks climbed into the Choctaw's wagon, and Bell flicked the reins and clicked his tongue. They moved south. When they reached the South Canadian River, the water level of which had dropped by this time, they crossed it into Pittsburg County.

They traveled without incident to a home outside of McAlester, where they met another Choctaw who conducted them to a place near the Kiamichi Mountains in southeastern Oklahoma in the old Choctaw Nation. A full-blood Indian man stepped out of the small house and smiled.

"This is another Daniel," said Daniel Bell, "but his name is Daniel Bob."

Daniel Bob held a hand out toward Chitto Harjo. "Welcome to my home," he said, speaking in Choctaw. "You'll be safe here."

1913

Fred Barde was anxious. His job as reporter for the *Guthrie Daily Leader* did not always provide him with exciting stories to work on. He had investigated the story of the Crazy Snake Rebellion a couple of years earlier, and he had never been satisfied that the story had really been resolved.

Therefore, he was excited when Jerry Samuel, a full-blood Choctaw Indian, had come to him to say that he had information about Crazy Snake. Barde had agreed immediately to accompany Samuel to a home out near the mountains.

They took a wagon, and the ride seemed to Barde to take forever.

"Where are we going?" he asked Samuel, who was driving the team.

"Daniel Bob house," was all the answer he received. Samuel's English was none too good, so Barde simply rode in silence for the rest of the trip. When they finally arrived, Daniel Bob was waiting in the rear. He had three chairs sitting there. He stood to greet Samuel and to be introduced to Barde. Then he motioned to the chairs, and they all sat down.

"He don't talk English," said Samuel.

"Well, ask him what he has to tell me," said Barde.

Samuel spoke briefly in Choctaw to Daniel Bob.

Bob sat up straight and cleared his throat. Barde perched on the edge of his chair, notebook and pencil in hand. Daniel Bob started to speak. It was not a long speech, and when it had become obvious that he was finished, Barde turned anxiously to Samuel.

"What did he say?" he asked.

Samuel then drew himself up and cleared his throat. "Here what he say. 'There was a man by the name of Chitto Harjo were came over here at my place. He were stay here while, and he got down in April 5, 1911, and the last few days of his life were spent in bed. One morning in April 11, he get down that with indeed distress, as the gunshot wound in his hip, and had died. Then we laid him good in my house yard. That where he lie in grave. That is all about Chitto Harjo death at my place.'"

"The Crazy Snake Rebellion" was over at last.

Not long after the news broke, two old Creek full-bloods sat on a bench beneath the branches of a spreading oak in the lawn of the Creek national capitol in Okmulgee. A younger man, perhaps in his thirties, sat in the grass in front of them, listening intently to their conversation. The old men were talking about things the younger man had only heard about, but they had taken part in the events of which they spoke.

They talked about the days they had spent at Hickory Ground with Chitto Harjo, and the time they had camped at Nuyaka with Isparhecher. And they told some thrilling tales about the flight to Kansas with Opothle Yahola.

The younger man listened with fascination and with respect, but when the old ones paused a moment, he spoke up. "Did you hear about that Choctaw man who said that Chitto Harjo died down at his house and he buried him there in his yard?" he asked.

"That's not true," said one of the old men. "They just told that story so the laws would leave him alone."

"You mean he's not dead?" asked the young man.

"No," said the other old man. "Chitto Harjo's not dead. He left here headed south, and he just kept on going. I imagine he's someplace way down in Mexico right now, taking life easy."

"Really?" said the young man.

"That's right," said the other old-timer. "He's in Mexico, and he's all right."